The
Guardian Angel
Project

BY TED WILLIAMS

DORRANCE
PUBLISHING CO
EST. 1920
PITTSBURGH, PENNSYLVANIA 15238

This is a work of fiction. Names, characters, places, and incidents are either the product of the author's imagination or are used fictitiously, and any resemblance to actual persons, living or dead; events; or locales is entirely coincidental.

Dorrance Publishing Co
585 Alpha Drive
Pittsburgh, PA 15238
Visit our website at *www.dorrancebookstore.com*

ISBN: 979-8-89341-191-1
eISBN: 979-8-89341-690-9

The Guardian Angel Project

INTRODUCTION

LIFE GOES ON AND THINGS HAPPEN ALL AROUND YOU.
YOU THINK, "IT CAN'T HAPPEN TO ME".
THIS IS ABOUT THE ONES IT DID HAPPEN TO.

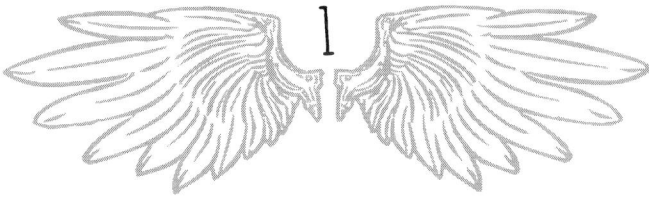

1

"BEN & JOE"

Their names are like any that you come across in everyday life.

You pass by them on the sidewalks, share small talk at the gas station, fight over a foul ball at the game, and I will bet you may even pray with them on Sunday.

Nothing they do seems out of the ordinary; they both are married, go to work every morning, mow their yards on the weekend and even share small talk over a cold beer talking about the football game.

Ben is in real estate, heads up the annual Christmas food drive for the church they attend.

Ben's wife, Jill, works at the local bank as a teller. She enjoys reading and gardening.

Joe is the local high school coach and social studies teacher.

Joe's wife, Mary, works as a substitute teacher at the local grade school. She enjoys painting and sewing; she is even won a few contests for her artistic skills.

Neither have any kids but it seems there will be lots of time for all that later.

They also do not receive many visitors related or not.

Both couples moved into the neighborhood relatively close just a few weeks apart.

As all good neighbors do, they snoop around when new families move into the neighborhood, checking the furniture and belongings of their newfound neighbors; all looked nice, not too fancy but comfortable, you know.

They hit it off almost overnight and start sharing their lives.

Joe and Ben spend a lot of time outdoors, golfing, fishing, hunting, camping, hiking, just about any excuse to get out would best describe them both.

Ben and Jill have some nice toys, a new fully decked out 4x4 Suburban that he pulls a long, beautiful toy hauler that has everything you can get including satellite dish, flat screen TV, outside wet bar, and a generator with enough power to light up a small city.

Down comes the back ramp and he has an array of custom motorcycles and quads to fill it up.

When these two did something, they did it to the fullest of enjoyment; their excitement had the neighborhood buzzing just watching them prepare for their outing.

One such weekend, Ben and Joe planned a hiking trip down into Big Bear Canyon to do some late season trout fishing before Old Man Winter moves in for the long haul.

It was like watching two kids in a candy store as the two prepared for their trip.

Getting all their gear accumulated, which always included a bottle of snake bite oil, good old sour mash whiskey, the best Tennessee had to offer.

The other neighbors joked and laughed at the two, maybe just a little envious perhaps!

The day came and both had arranged to leave work early enough to get a start around noon or so.

Even though it was a hiking trip, they threw all their gear in the back of the toy hauler.

Ben said, "Let's take it, and if we fish out or climb back out to late to make it home, we can get a good night's sleep before driving back."

The three-hour trip to the trail head flew by as they talked about all that they would be doing for the next few days.

They arrive at the kickoff point just above the trail head.

The air is crisp and slightly takes your breath away.

From off in the distance, you can just get a whiff of a campfire.

Autumn is really starting to take hold with the sun streaming down through the surrounding trees and bushes lighting up with all colors of the rainbow, what a sight, what a magnificent creation, truly heaven sent.

The two gather up the needed supplies and gear but before heading down the trail and like at most National Park Trails, there is a visitor sign in book where you state your name, how long you intend to be gone, when you intend to return, and an emergency number with a contact name just in case of some misfortunate mishap.

The two started down the trail descending deep into the canyon and taking in all that it can dish out.

The scent of pine trees was abundant, and wildlife was all around them as they go deeper into the canyon.

In the distance they could just start to hear the creek running through the canyon as they made their long descent down, deeper and deeper, leaving all of the city noise and problems behind them.

It was just getting dark when they arrived at their favorite fork in the creek where they had camped before, just a bit off the normal trail.

Their camp was very compact, one small tent, a few cooking utensils, a coffee pot, and just a few more essentials.

Both men had no problems falling asleep while listening to a Bull Elk bugling far up the canyon.

The next morning Ben awoke to find Joe gone; he was already walking up the creek fishing away. Ben knew what might be in store for both if Joe could catch a few fish, what a breakfast they would have.

Ben just laid there for a while taking in all the early morning sounds and smells.

The creek was just a few feet away, freely flowing down through the canyon.

Chipmunk's barking as they stand on guard for any predators that may be in lurking in the area.

Like most, first thing in the morning, the call of mother nature came over him; he had to take a leak, so he rolled out, gave a big stretch, and headed for the nearest tree.

With all personal matters taken care of, his first order of business was to brew up some fresh coffee. He walked down to the creek, scooped up a full pot of creek water. He paused for a second while glancing down creek, caught sight of Joe reeling in a nice trout.

He thought to himself and chuckled, I wonder if it is true about water being purified within fifty feet or so in a creek, setting the coffee pot down as he bent over to rinse his hands in the cold creek water.

Ben walked around the camp site picking up what he would need to start a fire. He collected some dry leaves which, with fall around the corner, were abundant. Next some small twigs which have fallen off through the summer through the rainy season, finally larger pieces of branches that he broke off a couple feet apart.

He looked around for the location of the fire pit they had made the last trip down. Not seeing it, he started dragging his foot over the leaf laced ground, his foot stopped, he bent down and found the rocks they had made a small circle for a fire pit. He brushed back all leaves and twigs about a couple of feet around, realigned the rocks that were out of place, and in no time had a nice fire going and the coffee brewing.

There was a large tree that had fallen, with all the leaves padding the ground, and some that were windblown up against the base of the fallen tree, it made a great place to sit, lean back, and take in the heat from the fire.

He did just that, and even though the morning air next to the creek was almost freezing, the warmth of the fire was mystical almost, warm, and soothing.

The coffee started to perk over. Ben repositioned it away from the fire; the steam sent the aroma downstream on a wisp of a breeze. Ben knew Joe would not be too long a coming.

Joe did get that aroma of a freshly brewed pot of coffee, reeled in one more trout and with that, headed back to camp. He did not even miss a stride dropping his gear and snatching up a cup. "Let me at some of that good old JO."

"Hold on," said Ben, "let's doctor up that coffee a bit on this cold morning." He reached into one of the packs and pulled out some sour mash whiskey, poured a good slug of it in both cups, then poured what room was left, filling the cups to the brim with coffee.

"Now that is a cup of JO," Joe replied after taking a big swig.

Kicking back and relaxing, Ben spoke up, "Guess I'll get the frying pan and get cooking the trout up, if you'll clean them," looking at Joe and smiling.

Joe took another sip. "Well now, I had thought about that long before you crawled out of your bag.

"I figured you would be wanting some breakfast, so I had them cleaned already before I came back, except the last one. I'll go clean it up while you start getting that frying pan hot."

Ben had a favorite pan for sure, an old cast iron that had been his dad's favorite pan for years when they used to camp out.

The pan had been used so much that it looked like shiny black glass. Nothing would stick to it, and cleaning it was no more than rinsing with some creek water and a little sand.

Ben set the pan on some hot coals and from a small bottle, squirted a little oil around the inside.

Joe, hearing the sizzle when the first trout hit the pan, hurried to clean the last fish.

The two men enjoyed a well-deserved breakfast of fresh cooked trout and eggs they had packed in, what a meal it was, and they both savored every bite.

Not sure if it is the altitude, mountains, creek, or just being outdoors. The food tastes different; anything you cook is great.

They were, as we say in camp, sitting around and telling lies of old glory days, just enjoying their company and being outdoors.

While they were relaxing, Ben noticed another angler coming upstream, ever so slowly but none the less Ben yelled out, "Hey, buddy, come on over and have a cup of coffee!"

The man hesitated but then shrugged his shoulders and yelled back, "Why not."

He came up the embankment, smiling as he reached out to shake the two men's hands and introduced himself, "Hi, I'm Frank. Boy I could smell your guys' cooking from half a mile away, especially that coffee."

Joe asks Frank, "Would you like to share in our fish breakfast? It would only take a minute to get one fried up for you," but Frank looking totally satisfied said, "No thanks, but if you have some medicine to add to that coffee that would be the ticket," smiling.

Ben and Joe laughed as Joe pulled the bottle from his jacket saying, "Just happen to have some right here."

The three shared small talk while finishing up sipping coffee and nibbling on the remaining fish.

Frank finished his coffee, looked up, shaking the last drops onto the ground, and said, "Well I best be getting along. Sure do thank the two of you for your hospitality."

They replied, "Our pleasure."

While he bent over laying his cup down by the fire, he rose, pulled a pistol from his pocket, and shot both men.

Frank looked around to be sure no one was near and might had witnessed his gruesome act, then he walked up to each man, first Ben, shooting him again directly in the head and saying, "That was for the millions you stole from us."

Then walking over to Joe and delivering another shot into his head says, "Sorry, buddy, wrong place, wrong time."

Frank wiped down the cup he drank from and put it back into the duffle bag. Picked up every spent casing, four total. He then packed the two men into their sleeping bags and put them in the tent.

While he was brushing away his footprints, he heard a sound from up the trail, ducting behind a tree being ever so silent awaiting who or whatever was coming.

After a short time, he took a glance around the tree only to see a raccoon coming down the trail more than likely had got wind of the cooking fish and was coming in for an easy meal.

He finished up and headed out of the canyon back to the trailhead and his vehicle.

2

"THE COUPLE"

Larry and Sue lived just outside the city in a small modular home.

Nowadays, you know it is not politically correct to say trailer anymore, but none the less it was home to them.

Larry was a struggling contractor taking on any job, big or small, that came along just to make ends meet.

Like most struggling companies, he was looking for that one project that would set him up, give him a real kick start into being a successful businessman, and contractor, a project we call, with some real teeth.

Larry had been dealing for weeks with some businessmen on a new shopping mall just inside the city limits. Many long hours of meetings, redrawing plans, trips to the city permitting office, and the endless going over and over the pricing and scheduling.

One day, almost dark, after working on a small remodel, he decided to stop by his office and check his e-mails to see if the guys for the shopping mall had sent any other requests for him to deal with.

As he hurried into his office, hoping to clean up any last-minute items quickly to get home at a decent hour so he might have a meal and some time with Sue.

Just as he was about to sit down, looking over the edge of his desk, he noticed an envelope laying on the floor by the mail slot.

Curious, he thought, as he walked over, picked it up; it was from the mall businessmen.

He thought about at first just tossing it over on his desk and dealing with their requests in the morning. As he made his way back to his desk, he opened it up, pulled out a folded letter, and a check fell from it. The note said, "Congratulations on being chosen as the successful contractor for the new mall."

This was quite the unusual way to find out, but so far, the whole experience with these guys had been less than usual.

He reached down to pick up the check; as he flipped the check over, he saw the dollar amount, two hundred and fifty thousand dollars. Larry fell back into his chair just staring at the numbers. Collecting his thoughts, he just couldn't believe what just happened.

Tilting back, with a big smile and a huge sigh of relief, he sprung to his feet.

He could not wait to get home to Sue to tell her the great news.

This project meant he could finally build her the dream home he promised and planned the past four years.

He was in a total brain fog all the way home, running the last few hours through his head, still not believing totally it was really happening.

When he arrived home, Sue was not there, not unusual but he was so excited he was about to bust a gut!

Sue finally returned home and seeing Larry's truck was filled with a warmth of knowing she could share some time with him and give him a good meal instead of warmed up and dry dinner he had been accustomed to from getting home so late.

Opening the front door and seeing Larry she asked, "What's up and why the mischievous grin on your face?"

Larry looking at Sue thought, how lucky am I to have such a beautiful woman and man she is glowing tonight smiling and so full of love. He replied, "What's up with you and what have you been up to?"

Sue, just coming from the doctor and finding out she was pregnant, did not know how to tell Larry. Her only thought was how hard he has been struggling and thought maybe the additional costs of bringing a baby into their lives at this time might not be a good thing, so she replied, "Oh nothing, how was your day?"

Larry could not stand it anymore and blasted out, "WE GOT THE NEW SHOPPING MALL PROJECT!"

He then started his two-step victory dance.

Sue, completely caught off guard, just blasted out, "GOOD I'M PREGNANT!"

Larry still doing his victory dance slowed, swallowed hard and looked at Sue and asked, "You're pregnant?" And in all his manly wisdom, paused then asked, "How did that happen?"

Sue fired right back, "The milkman, dummy!"

They both just stared and then grabbed each other and hugged like they were the only two on earth and right at that moment, they were.

That night's dinner, as you could understand, was the best they had in months; they both cooked up their favorite dishes for each other and talked all the while enjoying every second.

They were having such a good time they had not noticed that it was well past midnight.

Larry with a smile on his face said, "Miss Sue, you need to get your sleep, you know you are sleeping for two now."

Sue replied, "Yes and you, Mr. Contractor, have a big day tomorrow starting your new shopping mall."

Everyone can recall as a kid or heck even as an adult the night before Christmas, you try to sleep but just cannot do it. This is the night the two of them had, tossing, and turning, glancing at the clock every fifteen minutes.

When the alarm went off, they sprang out of bed eager to get with it, the first day of the rest of their lives.

Sue worked part time at a local day care center helping with the infant children, checking them in and helping through the lunch hour, then once they went down for their afternoon naps, she would leave.

Today she had a special stop to make, the local baby shops she had passed by for years on her way to and from the day care center.

Now she was driving by but stopping and looking at all the cute stuff in anticipation of what was to come; she can shop now for what was to be.

Sue thought after leaving one of the stores, on her way home, what would be a good thing for her and Larry do before he started his new project and got too busy, wouldn't be able to get away and with, she in a short time, will be too big to get away.

It had to be something they both enjoyed doing together; she thought about this all the way home.

Larry's day started as the day before ended, a bit strange.

His office was a converted large storage container which he converted into a quite a nice office on one end and storage in all the remaining.

He did this so if or when he got a large enough project, he could relocate it to be onsite office during construction.

As he pulled into his parking lot, he noticed some vehicles parked out front, not so unusual.

As he entered his office, he immediately saw the men for the shopping mall sitting around with the addition of someone he had never seen before.

Larry thought to himself how odd that somehow, they had entered his office even though he thought he had locked it last night, oh well maybe in all the excitement he had forgotten to lock it up.

He walked up and shook each man's hand and thanked each one for this incredible opportunity.

The odd man out came up and introduced himself simply as Bill.

Chuck was the kingpin for the group all along. Ben was always with Chuck, and without hesitation said, "Bill is an accountant and we thought with such a large project you could use the help with invoices, banking, payables, payroll, and all other day to day office items that go along with being a successful contractor like yourself."

Larry, still floating about a foot off the ground, came back down to earth, was quick to ask, "To be honest I had not put much thought into that yet, but how much is this service going to cost me?"

Chuck and the others chuckled, and Chuck responded, "He comes with the project; his salary is already taken care of."

Larry still confused a bit commented, "Well you can't beat that deal."

Larry was thinking all the while, so this is how successful people must feel like, and pulled his shoulders back and had a little taller stance and swagger about him.

Bill then stated, "They have been running you ragged for the past months, and we want you to take some time off and relax before you start."

Larry denied saying he had way too much to do getting the project out of the ground.

Chuck came over to Larry, put his arm around him, and said, "Son, all of that can wait, take some time off. Bill will start getting things organized while you are gone so take a few days and enjoy."

Larry was still not feeling comfortable leaving at such a critical time but agreed.

The drive home seemed to last for hours, Larry having so many things to think about with all that has happened in the last few hours and days.

He arrived at home after spending the better part of the day going over a few items before leaving with Bill, so he could get things organized.

He walked in the door, Sue grabbed him, gave him a big bear hug, and said, "Let's go camping!"

Larry gave her a big kiss and with a smile and not even saying a word, she knew he meant you bet!

They grabbed what gear they had and stopped at the local grocery store for some essentials they would need for a couple of days of camping and hiking.

After a few miles down the road and not saying much the entire time, Larry said, "Well, Sue, now that we have left, we better figure out where we are going!

They both laughed until tears rolled down their cheeks, happy tears.

Larry, wiping his face and still chuckling, had heard of a place a few hours away and with that told Sue, "I have just the spot to go."

He told Sue, "Relax, and take a nap," but she was too excited to do either.

They arrived, and with just enough light to hike down a short distance to a camp site. Set up their tent, grabbed a quick bite for dinner and sacked out for a good night's sleep.

With their newfound family and business to look forward to, their future was very bright indeed.

They awoke to the sound of the running creek water a short distance away. They sat and just smiled as they enjoyed a quick breakfast bar and some cool creek water before heading out on their day's journey.

Not having anything planned out, they just started walking.

After a hike down a path that followed the creek.

Stopping to watch some chipmunks play around a fallen oak tree, Larry, some distance ahead of Sue, took a few more steps but stopped. He thought he could hear some voices downstream. Looking back at Sue playfully watching the chipmunks, he walked down the trail just a short distance as the voices got louder. He stopped, turned back, and returned to Sue. He casually told her of someone just down the trail and thought it would be the neighborly thing to do and stop by and say hi.

They both gathered up their packs and started to walk. Sue's shoelace came undone and stopped to re-tie it.

Larry stopped and turned towards Sue.

They heard what sounded like large branches breaking and falling to the ground.

Still not knowing what it might be, they turned to walk down the trail, took only a few steps, looking up stopped, and with astonishment saw a man standing, pointing a gun at two men lying on the ground.

Larry did not hesitate, grabbed Sue, and fell into a close-by oak thicket, just off the trail.

They both laid there not making a sound. Larry raised up to see and heard the noise again. He knew now it was not branches breaking.

He was witnessing one man shooting the other two already lying on the ground. Larry fell back down alongside of Sue.

They laid in the thicket trying not to breathe; laid ever so quietly, not to be noticed or heard.

Every so often they could hear noises from the direction of the shooting but stayed ever so still.

After what seemed to be hours, Larry told Sue to stay still and that he was going to look.

He ever so slowly raised up, looking in the direction of the shooting, all he saw was a tent and a smoldering fire, so Larry turned grabbed up Sue and like two deer on the run, headed back to the truck, not an easy run being almost all uphill.

Just before topping out Larry stopped, catching his breath, tells Sue, "Hide here in these bushes while I go ahead to be sure no one was around." He slowly made his way to the top of the trail just staying off it a bit so not to be detected if anyone was waiting. In the parking lot, all he saw was a toy hauler hooked up to a Suburban and a couple of trucks, one being Larry's.

Larry ran back to help Sue up the last climb to the truck where they quickly tossed everything in the back and headed out.

The drive home was a quiet one with neither speaking a single word, both still shaking from what they had witnessed.

Sue was the first to break silence and asks, "Larry, what should we do?"

Larry not really knowing what to say or do just shrugged his shoulders with a blank look on his face, as if to say, I do not know!

After driving for a while and needing a rest, they came upon a truck stop.

Feeling safe with all the activity around a truck stop, they figured to grab a bite to eat and rest a bit for the rest of the trip home.

It had been quite some time now since they saw this horrible thing and silence still hung over them as they tried to force food down. Nothing really tasted good, just going through the motions.

The restaurant was almost full, not a lot of couples, mainly truck drivers.

They felt a little out of place but safe.

Sitting at the counter seats were a couple of truckers.

Larry overheard them talking. One said, "Wonder what's up about the shooting down in Bear Canyon, just a few hours ago."

He listened intensely to hear if anyone had witnessed the killing or any information about who may have done it.

The trucker says, "A game and fish officer came upon a tent that had two men in sleeping bags, both shot, he called in reinforcements immediately."

Sue overheard the truckers as well, feeling the emotional stress from the past, and hearing of it through the truckers talking, broke down and started to cry.

Larry, not wanting to draw attention to them, gathered her up, threw down double the amount of money to pay for their meal.

Holding Sue up, he headed for the door, as the truckers glanced at them walking by, noticing Sue being upset.

A few steps from the door, Larry looked out of one of the large windows and noticed a sheriff's car pull up. The waitress at the cashier counter remarked loudly, "The Sheriff is back from the canyon."

Like broadcasting it to everyone in the restaurant.

A huge figure of a man came from the car and entered the restaurant. The waitress asks, "How is it going, Sherriff?"

He replies, "Oh, we have a hell of a mess out there, not just the two men, but some poor soul drove off the side of a mountain. They are going down to get him out now, not sure if anyone survived the crash or not."

As Sue and Larry tried passing by him, he must have noticed that Sue was upset and still whimpering.

With a gentle hand he laid it on her shoulder, stopping her and asked, "Ma'am, is everything ok?"

She froze in place, not knowing what to do or say. She slowly nodded, looking directly into his eyes. "Yes."

The Sherriff replied, "Well, you sure look like you saw a ghost," smiling with that concerned look.

Sue could not hold back and broke down completely falling to her knees.

The Sheriff catches her, picks her up, carries her back towards a room the Elks Lodge uses for their monthly gatherings.

Telling everyone else to clear out, looking deep into Larry's eyes and putting his exceptionally large finger in Larry's chest and saying, "Except you!"

Even though he was a large man, he set Sue down ever so lightly saying, "There, there, it is ok," and he hands her his handkerchief.

The Sheriff quickly rose up and looked directly at Larry then asked, boy, "Are you going to tell me what is going on."

Larry did not say a word but looked directly at him. "Yes, sir."

He started recalling what happened today from when they started walking down the trail, seeing the horror of the killing of two men.

Running out as fast as they could to drive, ending up here at the truck stop.

The Sheriff says, "Stay here and do not talk to anyone."

As he leaves the room, he stops and tells one of the truckers standing outside the door, "Stay here and let no one inside this room, I will be back shortly."

For the next few hours, the truck stop turned into a Mecca of law enforcement and other types of agencies.

FBI, federal marshals, medical, and a small army of local law enforcement merged on the scene.

After what must have felt like hours of constant questioning from every agency on site, Larry asked for some time, for Sue and him to wind down a bit. They reluctantly agreed.

A strange thing happened after a short break; as they walked back from the restrooms, they tried to separate Larry and Sue.

Larry went into a rage grabbing Sue and letting everyone know they would have the fight for their lives on their hands if they tried to pursue this separation further.

Hearing the commotion, the masses separate.

In walks the Sheriff, walking between everyone and putting his hand on Larry's shoulder. He told him in a very reassuring way, "Settle down, it will be ok. You go with these boys, and I will go with Sue. I will not let anything happen to our girl."

Larry not feeling scared by his size but feeling comfortable leaned over to the big man and told him in an incredibly soft voice, "Sue is pregnant, take care of both for me, please."

The Sheriff just winked, nodded, and took Sue off clearing anyone within three feet of her—to be sure she was not touched in anyway.

Larry watched as the door shut behind Sue and then he was escorted off to another room.

Hours passed, questions flew faster and faster from what seemed every direction. Questions before they could even answer the ones already thrown at them.

To say the least, both were totally mentally and physically exhausted.

Just like a light switch, it all started to wind down and Sue and Larry where reunited.

A very refreshing few minutes of calm passed when a very well-dressed man approached them, Sheriff at their side.

As the man approached, the Sheriff stepped in front of the man and asked, "What are your intentions here, boy?"

The man stopped, introduced himself as FBI Agent Bernard Fyfe, showing him his badge. Everyone looked around as if to ask, "Is this guy for real?" Bernard Fyfe, looking around, did not hesitate with an answer for what he knew would be the next questions, and said, "Yes, Barnie Fyfe."

They all laughed for the first time which seemed like in days but none the less it was good to lift everyone's spirits a notch or two.

"Well, Agent Fyfe," asked the Sheriff, "what is your role in all of this?"

Agent Fyfe responds, "I head up the Division of Organized Crime in this region."

That could not be good, Larry thought to himself.

Agent Fyfe says, "I believe both Larry and Sue are completely telling the truth, and both identified the same man from hundreds of photos they had gone through over the past few hours."

Fyfe nods to the Sheriff to come his way. Larry speaks out, "You need to tell us as well, we have been through hell and deserve to know what is going on."

Fyfe pauses then says, "Now brace yourselves, it's not good. This man you claim you saw could be Frank Mast, the most dangerous hit man for the East Coast Families. He is one of the most wanted men by all law enforcement agencies nationwide, on the top ten most wanted as well as in quite a few foreign countries. He is only called upon for special assignments that require skills no other man has to offer."

Fyfe asked, "Would you be willing to testify if," pauses, "when we capture Frank Mast?"

Sue and Larry looked at each other all along knowing the right thing to do would be to testify, but Larry asks, "What would we be required to do and what kind of protection can you guarantee us if we do?"

Agent Fyfe replied, "Well first, whether you testify or not, please understand we must and will protect you."

The East Coast Families will more than likely put a contract out for both of you. Once the word gets out you witnessed the murders, Frank is worth more to them than your lives and they will do whatever it takes to see he stays out of prison or even captured.

Larry replies, "Well I guess that is what you call a no-brainer. Yes, we will testify," and so with that asked again, "What kind of protection program do you have for us?"

Fyfe says, "The most secretive program ever developed, so secretive that once the process starts, you will disappear and I will not even be able to find you, The Guardian Angel Project."

"What is all involved with this Guardian Angel Project?"

"We give you, prior to the arrest and trial, 24-7 round the clock protection, an undisclosed location of a safe house, for you to stay. Agents will be with you two as well as many more secretively watching, all around you until he has been brought to trial or has been eliminated."

Larry asks, "We will be placed into the Guardian Angel Project before or after trial."

Fyfe replies, "After you testify more than likely, and the verdict has been given."

"Kind of a funny name for something that represents so much bad," Larry commented.

"Well, I guess they look at that you guys as angels, and the project protecting you, so like a guardian angel watching over you two, just trying to do the right thing and help protect individuals from being harmed," replies Fyfe.

"Protect bad guys from Mast who probably deserve what they get in the long run anyway," Larry says.

"What did those two guys do so bad to deserve to die that way?" he asks.

Agent Fyfe replied, "Well I cannot tell you all the details, but I can tell you this, the Families believe that someone who steals money from them deserves nothing but to die if for no other reason, to show all others not to try to do the same."

Not too far from the truck stop was a small motel which for the short time being would be their home and headquarters for Fyfe and his agents.

By now Sue and Larry were so tired they could not comprehend what anyone was saying or doing, and the Sheriff says, "Let us get these folks down to the motel and let them get some well-deserved rest."

Not a day passed that the Sheriff did not stop by to check in on who he just called his girl; he also asked Larry now and again how he was doing as well, just to be polite.

Days went by. Sue and Larry started getting stir crazy cooped up in that little motel room not being able to go out and do any type of normal activity. It started to take a heavy toll on both, but through it all, they still had each other and that is what kept them strong and moving forward.

One day after some talk about maybe letting Sue and Larry go home, you see all the time agents had been staking out their home waiting, watching, phone taps, to see if any strange activity that might occur, but so far, nothing, so the day they were supposed to be able to go home, but still under complete protection Agent Fyfe arrived, they were ready.

Agent Fyfe, walking up, looking like someone had stolen his best puppy or worse, asks, "Do you think Frank ever saw you two?"

Larry was disgusted and replied, "For the ten thousandth time, no!"

Agent Fyfe looked down and looked straight into the couple's eyes and said, "We know that the East Coast Families have put out a contract for both of you. You both cannot go back home not even under total security and your life as you knew it," he pauses, "is over."

Sue looked at Larry and without even saying a word passes out!

Larry quickly grabbed her before she hit the floor; he cradled her in his arms and for the first time since all of this happened, holding her tight, he cried.

After cold compresses were applied, Sue slowly came to. She awoke to a frenzy of activity; all to protect her and Larry for what may lie ahead.

They were taken to a small private hanger at an airport where they boarded a jet, bound for where, they had no clue.

The jet taxied down the runway, made the turn for a takeoff approach and started the acceleration for takeoff.

Sue had sat at a window seat, and as the plane lifted off, she noticed a patrol car parked at the end of the runway and a large figure of a man standing next to it, the Sheriff. As the plane flew over, he looked up and fist held high as if to say, I will not let anything happen to my girl. Sue wept knowing she would never see her friend again.

They landed at a small remote airport, shuttled off in black Suburbans with blacked out windows. They had no clue where they could be.

The suburban stop and after a few minutes, both were escorted to the back door of a house.

The windows all had shutters that blocked out the light. The doors from the inside looked like all steel with multiple locks.

It was a mini fortress, built to stop any type of easy access.

It was very comfortable, and no provisions were spared, they asked, and it appeared soon after.

The one thing they needed but couldn't have: access to leave or even go outside.

They felt like they were prisoners themselves.

Weeks went by and Sue being pregnant started feeling some of the effects motherhood brings on.

Neither Sue nor Larry could not figure out where they were, what city, state, for that matter what country.

Not a day went by that she and Larry did not try to recall how could Frank have seen them and like all the other times in the past came up empty again.

One afternoon, Larry, being an outdoorsman and having no access to even go outside, started watching an outdoor channel on hiking.

On this one episode, the would-be hikers with their guides stopped at a boarder where the guards requested information about them, where they planned to hike, how long they would be out in the field and then return, and an emergency contact name and number to call, just in case.

A chill came over Larry and he stood up and ran out of the room, ran down the hall leading to an outside door and was met by two agents before he could exit.

The agents had grown fond of their two companions and knew by Larry's action that he was deeply disturbed about something.

The agents' first thought: something is wrong with Sue.

Larry said in an excited voice, "I know how Frank knows who we are!"

One of the agents immediately called Agent Fyfe and in a matter of a few hours he was with Larry and Sue.

Fyfe asked, "What is this about Frank?"

"I know how he knows," Larry replied.

"Ok, go on, tell me how he knows," ask Fyfe.

"The log-in book at the head of the trail, you know the one you write your name in and how long you plan to be and all that."

Sue looking pale goes down to her knees, looking up says, starting out slowly, "And leaves an emergency name and number in case something happens, oh my God, oh my God!"

Larry asks, "Sue, what's wrong?"

She replies in a frightened voice, "We put my sister's name, Tami. We put Tami's name and information on the list. We must protect Tami!"

Fyfe not wasting any time gets more information about Sue's sister and sends a full SWAT team over to her house.

Sue yells out, "Give me a cell phone so I can call her!"

Fyfe tells Sue, "Give Tami's phone number to an agent."

"No," she replies, "I must call her now," getting hysterical.

"No Sue, you must give us her number and now."

Sue reluctantly tells them her number weeping while saying the last few numbers.

The agent tries to call her.

"Why can't I call her?" Sue asks.

Fyfe replies, "Frank may be listening and may try to trace the call back to find you." The agent gets only a recording that her message box is full and cannot accept any more messages.

Everyone's mood intensifies in expectation that something evil may have found Sue's sister.

Her sister lives alone in a nice colonial style home in an incredibly quiet neighborhood.

The agents and SWAT team arrive to newspapers cluttering the porch and the mailbox full of letters.

The SWAT team having the home surrounded first knock, and then ring the bell, call out for Tami with no response at all.

They open the screen door to see if the main door was open; it was not, locked from the inside.

The back door and all windows were checked, and all was in place and locked.

Agent Fyfe, who was in constant contact with the captain in charge of the SWAT team, ordered them to blow the hinges off the door and enter the premises.

The captain paused and said, "What about a search warrant?"

Fyfe responded, "On my authority and the possible chance of foul play, I give the order to blow out the damn door, now do it!"

Fyfe heard the three blasts from the riot gun and then the noise of the SWAT team entering the home and a house alarm going off.

Agents yelling "FBI" as well as SWAT team members yelling "Police Department."

After a few minutes, everything quiets down and the captain comes back on the phone with Fyfe.

"Sir," the captain says, "the only thing we found was a hungry cat, nothing else, but evidence of a home that had been unoccupied for some time." He told him of the mail and newspapers.

Fyfe immediately declared the home a crime scene and ordered every inch of it gone over.

Now for the most difficult part for Fyfe, telling Sue, he had, like everyone else around Sue and Larry, become quite found of them both, almost family like.

As Fyfe entered the room where they had been waiting, he said, "The house appeared to be unoccupied for some time and all we found was a hungry cat."

"Tami was not there?" Larry asks.

"Just a hungry cat," Fyfe lowering his head replied.

"Tami has a cat, and she would never leave it unattended if she knew she would be away for any length of time," Sue says.

Fyfe asks Sue, "Was she planning a trip?"

"Not that I know, she would be sure her cat was taken care of," Sue says in a disturbed way.

Larry asked, "Did you call her before you left?"

Sue replied, "I tried and only got a recording, so I left a message, maybe that is how Frank found out, and he accessed her voicemail."

Fyfe asks, "Do you know who Tami worked for so we can contact them and find out if they know her whereabouts?"

"Sure, it is the Moore Travel Agency."

Fyfe instructed an agent to investigate this ASAP.

Fyfe being in the FBI for years and understanding though this is normal for him it is putting a toll physically and mentally on both Sue and Larry.

He said, "I have been around you two for quite a while now but outside what I have read in reports I really do not know either of you."

He knew that talking about something besides the killings and her sister would help relieve some tensions especially with Sue worried so much about her sister.

"Well, we were the only two children my mom and dad had." Sue pauses, slightly smiling, continues, "They wanted to keep trying until they had a son, but Mom got sick and had a miscarriage. They don't know if it was a girl or boy but soon after she had to have a hysterectomy."

"Sorry to hear that," replied to Fyfe. "How far apart are you two girls?"

Sue again pauses, reflecting, with a hint of a smile. "We are only a year apart."

"Are your parents still with us?"

"No, Mom and Dad were killed in an automobile accident while we were away at college."

"I feel for you both. What happened?"

"No one is sure, but they were returning from a weekend vacation and the car went out of control," Sue says, as tears start slowing go down her cheeks.

Fyfe quickly says, "What was it like in college with the two of you," and he hands her his handkerchief.

21

She takes a breath and wipes her face. "Tami and I, let's see, I am the oldest so I waited a year for her to get out of high school so we could both go to college together."

Fyfe replies smiling, "Bet you two were hell raisers."

She smiled reflecting back. "Oh I don't think so."

Larry steps in, "Now do not forget I was around. Who did they call Thelma and Louise!" laughing out loud.

"Ok we had a blast the first three years until the accident. We became inseparable those years before and especially after. When Mom and Dad died, we left school to take care of their affairs and never had a chance to go back." Sue paused as if floating back to a better place and time, freeing her for a moment from all the hell she has been going through.

Fyfe, recognizing her bewildered expression, asks, "Larry, how do you fit into all of this?"

Larry smirking says, "I was walking around campus one of the first days I arrived, just checking it all out. I was from a small town, so a university was a big deal, more people here than my entire hometown combined.

"I was walking up and just opening the door to the cafeteria when the door flung open and hit me knocking me back. Out walked these two girls just talking away and not noticing anything else around them or the fact they just knocked me on my ass. I cleared my head a bit and Sue slightly turned her head to see what the commotion was about. Seeing me, she just cracked a smile and kept walking and talking away."

Sue says, "That was you Larry? I had no idea. I remember that day and glancing to be sure no one was hurt."

"That's ok, I knew from that point on I was going to get to know you. If this wasn't love at first sight for me, I don't know what else it could be. I found out through a friend's girlfriend about these two sisters who had just started so I purposely waited outside your dorm for you to come out one day and made it a point to get you to notice me, remember?"

Sue covered her face with her hands, embarrassed maybe or covering up trying not to laugh out loud. "Who could forget that day, you nut! Well Tami and I were heading out to run and get some hair spray or something like that. As we walked by this huge tree outside our dorm, there was this guy hanging from his ankles from a large limb. We stopped, at first thought he was dead or something but then he opened his eyes and winked at us. We both laughed and I waved at him and went on. Later that day when we returned there, he was again, but this time he was standing on his head with his feet up against the tree. I told Tami I had to meet this guy and she said, 'I'm going up to the room, if you're not back in five minutes, I'm calling security,'" chuckling.

"Well, that was that. Sue came over and I asked her out on a date. Well things were a little complicated at times, the sisters were almost inseparable, making it a challenge for us to be alone. I knew I just couldn't have her stop her great relationship with her sister without causing some major issues. I took whatever time Sue and I had alone to get close to her. Never getting negative with Tami's presence. I just took it in stride, and we did everything, the three of us, together. To be honest, it was a blast, I had two beautiful girls, one as a friend and the other, well as a possible future wife.

"Later on one day when I stopped by the dorm, both her and Tami where gone. I asked around but could not find out why, all anyone knew is they had to leave for a family emergency. A few days later Sue calls me and explains the terrible accident about her parents. We both cried over the phone."

"Sounds like a solid relationship you two must have had," Fyfe remarks.

"Yeah, we stayed in touch while I completed college and when I got out I could not wait to relocate to Sue's hometown to be with her. Now with Tami having a full-time job, I got busy and courted Sue properly. We got engaged about a year later and moved into that crappy old trailer."

"Crappy old trailer," Sue blasted out, "that crappy old trailer was a palace to me because it was ours, and I love that trailer."

"I apologize, your majesty," Larry replies laughing.

Fyfe was laughing when his cell phone rang; it was the agent getting in touch with Tami's company.

"We have contacted the travel agency and they said they had not heard from her for several weeks, around the time of the killings. They too had tried to get in touch with her with no success."

Fyfe knowing this would disturb Sue gave a half smile to Sue and a wink and left the room as if to say, it is ok, do not worry, nothing could have been more from the truth.

Fyfe ordered the agent, "Look, we may have a possible kidnapping and another homicide on our hands, and we need something to go on so go back to the house and follow up on any possible lead no matter how small. Call the agency again and get her records of all clients and phone records. Something must give here, we are running out of time!"

Fyfe reentered the room and thinking to himself, what could I possibly tell Sue and Larry that will not upset them? Nothing, nothing at all.

He sat down, asked if someone could get him a glass of water and asked if anyone would like something to drink.

Sipping his water, he tried to come up with a way of letting them know what they found at the travel agency.

He looked at Sue and Larry sitting next to each other on a small couch.

The look in their eyes was one of possible hope, some small speck of good news to grasp onto.

He thought of something his dad told him many years ago.

One day, just a teenager, Fyfe remembers the day of his mother's birthday.

They were not poor but had to make ends meet whenever they could.

His dad told his son, "Let's go get your mother a nice gift."

Knowing his dad didn't have two nickels to rub together, he had no idea what he was going to buy.

Stopping at a house I had never been to, Dad opened the trunk and pulled out his grandfather's shotgun that he gave to him a few months before passing.

Walking up to the door, he knocked, knocked again.

The door opens and Jim, Dad's hunting buddy, says, "So you finally want to sell that gun I've been after you for years."

Jim starts handing Dad one-hundred-dollar bills, one right after another.

Seemed like Jim would never stop, but he did.

Never did ask how much, Dad never said neither.

Just smiled a bit, said thanks, and see you next time out hunting, waving as he walks down the walkway to the street.

Driving down the road leading to the main part of town, I could tell Dad was somewhere else.

He had a look of being somewhere else but was a good somewhere.

Stopping in front of the department store, he turned off the truck, looked straight ahead, and in a soft voice said, "Let's go get your mama something she's been dreaming about for years."

I asked, "Dad, how could you sell your granddad's shotgun?"

Like he said to me when he gave it to me, "To see someone else being happy."

"Your mama is going to be so happy with what we are going to get her."

"But Dad, she wouldn't let you sell your granddad's shotgun for any reason, you know that."

"I know, son, so we are going to tell her a little white lie and keep it to ourselves, and we'll feel good inside when we see you mama getting pleasure out of her gift, you okay with that?"

So, Fyfe, conjures up not the entire news about Tami, a little white lie included.

He just had to pass it on and make someone just a little happier, even for just a few moments.

3

"FRANK"

Frank is not your typical stereotypical hit man; he was what you would call a prodigy, one of a kind.

He had grown up like most in a small town just south of Dallas, Texas with his parents.

He was the only child his parents had. They were not wealthy but lived a comfortable life and loved their son greatly.

His parents never missed any of his many sport activities he ever was interested in doing.

He had lots of friends all through grade school and high school and graduated top of his class.

He was also from the very beginning a well gifted athlete, especially in football.

He had numerous colleges offering great full ride scholarships to play.

He was just a great kid, happy go lucky attitude, having fun and enjoying everything life could offer.

In his second year of college, being a left end on the football team, running down the sideline and doing a post pattern route, he went up high to catch the ball, which he did.

On coming down he was sandwiched between two defensive players, knocking the wind from his chest and the hard landing knocking him out cold.

On slowly recovering from the massive blow, he felt a sharp agonizing pain; he had suffered a career ending injury to his left knee.

After this, his happy go lucky attitude turned sorry, and one after another, his friends started to give him a wide path avoiding him at all costs, not wanting any type of association with him.

Something a true friend would not do, but a true friend would try to find out why such a mood and attitude change occurred. It couldn't have been just the injury causing this.

He even isolated himself from his parents. Any of their efforts to help him, he rejected and grew angrier as the weeks and months went by.

He started missing school, a day here, another day there until one day he stopped showing up all together.

He became a wanderer, homeless without any direction or hope for the future; he cared less about himself, whether he lived or died.

He would hitch hike up into the mountains and spend days away from any contact with anyone.

His parents gave up all hope of ever seeing him again after months of searching. Still hoping to see their son in the future.

One day while he was scavenging through some dumpsters for food behind a restaurant, in another city.

Another drifter also looking for food shoved Frank as he grabbed what was left of a sandwich, knocking Frank up against the dumpster and to the ground.

Frank hesitated for a moment and then this rage deep down inside him swelled up, a rage so fierce he had no control over his mental being.

He stood up, grabbed the first thing in reach which was an empty wine bottle.

He then stood up over the man who was bent over looking into a small trash can. With all his strength he wheeled the wine bottle and struck the man in the back of the head just above his shoulders, sending him to the ground, killing him instantly.

Frank stood over the man knowing he had just ended a life and was puzzled!

He should feel remorse, saddened over taking a life but instead he felt a rush that he had not felt for quite some time long before his knee injury in college.

He first checked the man's pulse to be sure he was dead.

Then after looking around to see if anyone had witnessed his act, he walked back over to the victim. He picked the man up and placed him into the large dumpster and left.

He also picked up the bottle and took it with him, dumping it quite a distance away, several blocks from the actual area he had killed the man.

For days he thought over and over not being able to sleep thinking about what happened and how he felt.

He isolated himself away from everyone and left town to avoid being suspected of this horrible act and has never returned.

He couldn't stop thinking about that rush he felt that day and how he couldn't shake it off.

He decided to pursue this feeling further by going out into the streets and doing whatever it took to get to the point that he could prosper, and have that feeling like he had that day.

He started to associate with the worst kinds of people, drug addicts, pimps, prostitutes, and drug dealers, the worst of the worst.

Until one day came an opportunity he had been waiting for, another chance to kill but this time for money.

A drug dealer approached Frank; he told him he had money stolen from him by one of his street dealers and wanted Frank to take care of him, to show an example to all others that he was one not to mess with. He told him he would pay him well.

Frank, thinking he did not want the dealer to think he was Mr. Eager Beaver, hesitated, kicked around some debris that was in the gutter, before agreeing to do the drug dealer's dirty work.

Frank set up a buy with the dealer and made sure other drug users knew and were around when it went down.

He knew that even if they witnessed him taking this dealer out, no one would believe anything the drug users would say being under the influence.

He set this all up in the back of an abandoned home that druggies used for taking drugs and hanging out, a flop house.

Surrounded by drug users and feeling quite safe, the dealer met Frank at the house.

Frank acted and looked the part wearing old torn clothes which wasn't hard seeing he had been wearing the same clothes for months now.

Sitting on an old broken couch in which was at one time, what might have been a living room.

As the dealer smugly approached, acting like he was doing Frank a huge favor selling him drugs, Frank rose from the couch and with one swipe cut the man's throat, nearly severing his head from his shoulders.

Everyone in the house fled without hesitation, well at least the ones that could.

Frank wiped any blood off him that he could see, put the rag in his pocket, and calmly walked out the front door and down the street.

His first hit rewarded him with five hundred dollars and the start of a reputation to be the guy you could call on to get it done.

Each time after, he was paid more than the last job.

The money Frank would be paid over the years was nothing to the feeling it gave him, the feeling of being alive while watching others die without knowing why.

He became a master of his trade, studying everything possible on how the human body reacts to drugs, chemicals, water, air, impacts, fire, explosions, electricity, weather, and on and on and on!

He became so efficient he could virtually pick up a handful of dirt and make an explosive from this powder, powerful enough to kill.

He knew exactly every weakness of the human body, that by applying pressure here or a little more there would rend them helpless or could kill.

He would study his victims for days, weeks, and months at a time watching and learning, waiting for that one tiny thing that he could use to give him that edge to end their life and he became known for best, making it look natural or by accident if possible.

To the underworld, money is everything and they live and die by it. The only thing held equally dearer was family, sacred ground not to be touched under any circumstances.

The underworld regulates itself, you buy, you use, you sell, almost anything imaginable, you screw up, you lose, plain and simple, end of story.

That is where people like Frank come into play and in Frank's world, once he is set into play, there is no returning, no stopping, he cannot be contacted in any way to end it once he has the green light, with a large deposit, to get a job done.

One of Frank's specialties was group killings, one of very few that could take on such a situation and come out with the results they wanted.

He was once contracted to take out a group of businessmen that had gotten away with millions, so they thought.

He did his research on all these men for weeks and flat could not come up with anything that linked them together, that one common denominator he could use against them.

One day he hit upon something that had happened once before.

He remembered a time some of the men would all meet the night prior to golfing to have dinner and drinks, interesting being that out of the four men, only three of them played golf but none the same, this was a time when all four were together.

Not having any set days they played golf, Frank waited and started formulating different plans based on different types of scenarios that may occur.

A few weeks later, Frank got a lead of the four men meeting up at their favorite steak house; it had to be the dinner before golfing.

His lead, he saw one of the four, walking out of a golf shop with a new putter in hand.

He knew how golfers cannot wait to try out new equipment and seeing they usually played golf monthly on the same day of the week; he must watch more closely before he took a shot in the dark on when. It would be that same day in a few days or weeks coming up.

Frank knew to hit four at a public place was not ideal or smart.

He already knew a few facts about the four men, so he did have some especially useful information to use.

One key thing he had discovered while watching them at a restaurant one afternoon, one of the four did not drink alcohol, maybe something he could use.

One day, around seven that night, the four men came in separate vehicles arrived at the steak house just outside a small suburban town.

It was a cloudy, rainy day with a forecast of the possibility of heavy thunderstorms throughout the area.

The four began their evening in the bar waiting for a table to be freed up for them.

It seemed a long time waiting for a table, but the drinks were great, and the service was spot on.

The bartender brought them drinks on the house feeling bad about the long wait. The four took it in stride, laughing and joking with the bartender.

Finally, the waiter with much relief escorted the men to a nice table by a picturesque window overlooking the city; it was a mother nature's light show with the storm moving through the area.

The waiter brought all another drink, another round on the house, thought they might tip him more for the courtesy he was showing them.

They all ordered up their favorite meals and had a very enjoyable evening, some not feeling much pain I might add.

As they started to get up to leave, loud thunder and a bright flash from a close lightning strike lit up the entire area and lights flickered in the restaurant.

They had not realized the thunderstorm had made its way so close while they were inside enjoying their meal.

The one who did not drink soon realized without much thought that the other three had well indulged themselves and were not in any condition to drive home especially in this weather, so like a good friend should do and with little resistance, he gathered up all their car keys.

"Okay boys, the ride home leaves in five, bottoms up," he says.

Well, that was the first of many "let's go boys" before the boys did finally leave.

The storm now fully developed and was dropping rain in sheets along with lightning so often you hardly needed headlights.

Slowly and squinting, pulling out of the restaurant parking lot they had to go in the opposite direction they came from with a solid center median in the road blocking any left turns.

So, they continued right out of the parking lot even after one of the men made a comment about just jumping over the median curb, one of the drunken ones of course.

"Damn, if this was a rental, we would give her a go for sure," all laughing.

Just before coming up to a traffic light that was not working, they noticed something large laying directly in front of them; a large tree had fallen over and had blocked the entire road. Not sure from the horrific wind and rain or a lightning strike.

Looking around for another way out, without turning around, the driver could barely see clearly but did notice that there was a small road just off to the right.

So down they went soon realizing that the roadway was just a back alley behind some buildings.

Slowly making their way and commenting on how bad the storm was, a gust of wind rolled a large trash can right in their path, having them stopping abruptly.

The four joked about what poor soul was getting out to move the trash can while the down pour was still raging, so they played a game of paper-scissor-rock. What else would four grown men do, and as you might guess, one of the intoxicated ones lost.

What a sight watching him slipping and stumbling around while the rain pounded him all the while. Lightning flashing like fireworks on the Fourth of July.

As he reached down to grab the trash can, a bright flash and loud explosion went off.

When it all cleared away, it looked like a war zone.

All four men lay dead outside, halfway out and still in the car.

Fire department, police, all came to this awful accident that had occurred.

The TV and newspaper reported a tragic accident the next day. Four men in a car had been struck by a fallen power line and were pronounced dead at the scene by the responding EMTs.

All four had been killed by Frank; the four men never knew that from the time they stepped into the restaurant they would be dead hours later.

Frank was the bartender who gave the men the great service, not by drugging but by giving them in free drinks, while waiting on a table, a restaurant that on a foul night was busy, but with the great service and free drinks they had not really noticed. He knew he had to get them all in one car without any suspicion. Frank had found out the most likely place for the golf dinner and had applied for a bartender's position, had been working for a week under a completely different identity. He even went back and kept working for some weeks after to shed no interest in himself, just another gypsy bartender going from place to place.

He had watched the weather report and did his own predictions on what might happen that night. He had purchased his own Doppler weather station.

He studied the routes in and out of the restaurant, slipped out sometime before the men left and toppled the tree with a charge of explosives to simulate a blown over tree, what the four men thought was a lightning strike nearby.

He knew they would turn down the alley so he days before dug out ruts deep enough so when filled with water the metal wheels would be in contact to conduct electricity throughout the vehicle.

He knew each car the men drove and had the dimensions to the non-drinker's car so to be very precise.

He knew of the high voltage wires above, set an explosive charge that would be mistaken for a lightning strike, rolled the trash can out and witnessed the man trying to move it.

Set off the charge that would have the high voltage lines fall directly on the car causing an explosion and killing all four.

To everyone around it was just a sad misfortune for four buddies going home from a night out at the steakhouse who happened to take a wrong turn at the wrong time.

But it was a premeditated, extremely calculated murder of four men, which is why Frank was the best; no one even looked past the obvious—electrical storm, down power lines, and four scorched bodies, case closed.

This is Frank, his life, his being and purpose on earth.

He could be the guy who offers you help with a flat tire, sits near you at the movie theatre, maybe the guy who installs your satellite dish, you would never know.

That is the way he wanted it, his victims not knowing.

Frank, after watching Joe and Ben for weeks, knew of their hike down Bear Canyon and set his plan in motion. He knew that being so late in the year that it would be truly little chance of many hikers being out, so he chose that trip to take care of Ben, Joe was a victim of chance.

Outside of being neighbors and friends, Joe knew little of what Ben did for a living and Ben hid his fortune well from everyone, even his own wife.

So, Frank parked down the road from the Trailhead and hiked down into the Canyon the day before waiting for the two men and watching for anyone else that may venture in at the wrong moment.

He did stroll up stream fishing away but was on the alert for any onlookers and you can be sure if anyone else was around he would have just kept walking by and wait for the next opportunity, he took his chance and Joe and Ben where killed.

Frank, being very thorough to the point of almost paranoid, went to the Trailhead and tore out the last page they had signed on and left information.

He also knew to use this to check for any remaining hikers down in the Canyon he didn't know of.

The list was short, Larry and Sue, Ben and Joe, and a single hiker who did not leave a name just a number but was still down in the canyon.

Larry and Sue must have been minutes ahead of Frank but did fail to check off that they had returned from hiking; if they had, he might not have come looking for them, but Frank knew he had to be sure to clean up all loose ends just to be sure so he looked into the parking lot and saw only one vehicle knew that someone had left without signing out, the single hiker or Larry and Sue.

With only two vehicles in the parking lot and one he knew was Ben and Joe's, the other had to belong to one of the remaining hikers.

Frank then cut the brake line just enough so under hard braking, they would fail.

He then took pictures of the vehicle so he would be able to recognize it coming or going.

He went down the road quite a way at a steep downhill grade that had a sharp turn at the bottom. After placing some specialized charges around the base of a large rock formation he waited. He did not have to wait long when the vehicle he remembered came down the road. Frank could tell whoever was driving was having trouble stopping it and right at the precise spot, Frank set off the charge and the rock formation tumbled down onto the vehicle taking it over a 100-foot embankment killing anyone inside.

Frank's single mistake, not crushing the vehicle on the road so to be able check its driver, miscalculated the force of the rocks, now he did not feel like he had enough time to climb down and check, so left and headed back into town.

As he approached the truck stop, he saw all the commotion encircling the truck stop, so he stopped for some gas and filling up he casually asked the attendant, "What is the commotion about?"

The attendant replied, "A guy and his girlfriend witnessed a shooting down in the Canyon and there must be twenty cops inside asking them questions."

Frank did what he does best and started preparing, gathering information, and patiently waiting for that right moment when they would make a mistake, expose them for just a second too long. He knew about Larry, Tami, Sue's sister, and contemplated on how best to utilize that pawn in his game of cat and mouse.

He knew with all the protection they had around the couple this one was going to be a long one. Frank smiled as he thought of it, smiling knowing the pleasure he would get out of the planning and all that would follow, especially the killing.

This was Frank's life, and he knew what was needed, clean up all loose ends and move on.

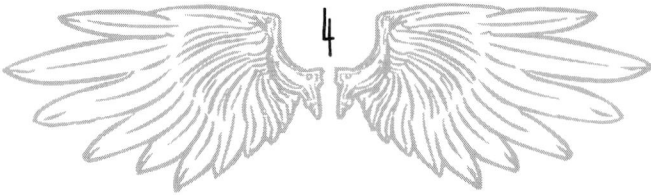

4

"THE SET UP"

It was sometime later when Frank received a contact from an associate they had another case for him to handle. Again, someone thought they could steal money and get away with it.

This time it was from within. An inside accountant, they suspected, started skimming some money for himself, so the contact was made to Frank to move into action.

Frank soon found out this accountant was double dipping, getting money to be an accountant but through some, let us say, very inventive accounting methods, was getting money from the folks who borrowed or used Family money for a project by inflating the interest or pay backs, paying the Family their share and keeping the difference. The Family caught on when an associate had made some complaints to a Family member which is a big mistake but did raise a few questions which they found the answers for very quickly, the accountant was double dipping.

This accountant was not only stealing from the Family but also was, to be kind here, a complete idiot! He was riding high with all the cash living like there was no tomorrow, and in a way, he was partly correct but did not know it at the time.

So, Frank started his surveillance on the accountant, following and watching his every move, waiting to find that one thing he could get him on. He found this guy to be an easy mark; he was flaunting money around like it grew on trees.

Frank's focus turned temporarily away from finding Larry and Sue while trying to finalize the contract on the accountant.

The one thing this guy was doing, every Thursday night he would hire an escort service and meet this lady of the night at a motel, the same motel simply different companions. She would leave, and he would stay until morning.

So here was the thing he was looking for. He would hit this guy at the motel sometime after his escort had left but early enough not to be around when the other motel travelers were making their way onto their next destinations.

Today was Monday and he had a bit of time to kill, sorry the pun, so knowing he had a real done deal, Frank decided to check up on Larry and Sue to see if there were any changes seeing he had been a few days since he last checked up on them.

Even though the security around them was airtight, Frank had managed through his sources to find out where they had the couple in seclusion. It did require for him to travel some distance between his new contract and the couple, but he figured he had the time, so it was worth the gamble.

It paid off big time. When he was just arriving at the couple's retreat, he saw three black Suburbans pull up. He thought this quite interesting, so he sat by watching closely. Next he saw what he knew had to be agents going in and out of the home. Then a funny thing happened, three sets of agents each escorting individuals who had been wrapped up all in black and each set getting into an individual Suburban and driving off. Frank knew it had to be Sue or Larry, which one he could not tell or which one it was, and which ones were the decoys. He stayed around not following any of the vehicles; he had no idea at this point which one might be the one, and so he hung tight to see when they would return. Frank knew it would be very suspicious and might raise some interest if the agents watching over the couple saw his car parked in one spot too long, so he moved around to different locations but still in view of the home.

The agents had picked a well located home seeing there were four different routes into the area as well as escapes routes; there were also two freeways within a mile of the home, so it was somewhat difficult for Frank to cover all

THE GUARDIAN ANGEL PROJECT

routes in and out. He thought at first to delete the route they had left in the morning but then thinking again thought if it was himself doing the protection, he might use the same route to confuse anyone watching.

Hours passed when one right after another Suburban pulled up and each of the wrapped individuals went back into the home, one after another about a minute apart.

Today was Tuesday so he knew he could hang for another day before heading back to take care of business with the accountant.

He knew just being in the area was exposing himself, so he had to come up with a way to be able to stay observing without himself being observed.

He had noticed a city manhole cover just down the street but in view of all routes in and out.

So, the next morning very early, he went down to the city maintenance yard looking for something he could use, and he hit on something that might work. He watched as the shift change occurred and slipped into the employee lounge and took a pair of overalls the city workers wore while working, then he went into the yard and found a van to use and drove out the gate waving at the guard as he went by. The guard waved back as if to say, have a great day.

Frank about wet himself laughing how he just walked in and drove out without a hitch.

He set up by the manhole even setting up the umbrella and small barricade around the manhole just like you would see almost every day, not paying any attention to what was going on.

He had been there for a couple of hours when two agents came from behind the house and made their way across the yard.

Frank thought nothing of it until the agents started walking directly towards him. Frank being the cool person under pressure just started playing the part of a city worker.

The agents walked up, one staying back as one approached Frank. He asked, "What is up here?"

Frank replied, "Oh how you doing, just doing an inspection. We have been getting some complaints about rodents, so they sent me down here to check around. You guys have not seen any have you?"

"Well how long will you be here?"

"Should only take another hour or two, why what is up?"

The two agents glanced at each other. "Can we see some identification please."

Frank reached like he was getting into his back pocket and then commented, "Damn, I left my wallet in my clothes back in my locker, but here is my city employee badge. Man I am sorry about this."

The agent took the badge and again looked back at the other agent. He said, "Well we would appreciate you packing up and leaving now if it would not be too much trouble."

Frank replied, "No not a bit, when would be a good time to come back?" he asked.

"Well, we will contact the city and let them know."

Frank reached out to shake the agent's hand and said, "Sure thing, these rats can wait for a while longer I guess, and I will be out of here in two shakes."

The agents returned to the house and Frank made a hasty retreat; everyone breathed a bit easier.

Frank dumped the van and headed back to his accountant realizing if the agents did contact the city and asked about the employee as well as the job, they would realize it had all been a bunch of bunk.

Frank realized that getting to these two was not going to be an easy task. He tried to put himself in their position, living like caged animals, never out of sight of an agent at any time, never having a quiet moment alone, going outside to enjoy the blue sky and warm sun was even out of the question, some kind of life. Here he was doing whatever he wanted, going anywhere he wanted to go and him the bad guy and these two normal citizens now imprisoned for just doing the right thing.

The toll of being stuck together was taking a toll on Larry and Sue. Weeks now months had gone by, Sue now getting bigger what seemed like hourly. It matched her disposition as well, she was becoming harsh towards Larry and especially all the agents.

Just think about it, how would you fair if you were stuck in a small house for weeks without being able to do one normal activity? You would go completely nuts!

Frank knew he could use this to his advantage somehow but not quite sure, so he stayed around.

The next morning Larry and Sue would get up whenever they were done sleeping which seemed to grow longer and longer to just sleep boredom away.

THE GUARDIAN ANGEL PROJECT

Sue went to make some scrambled eggs and noticed that the agents had brought their usual groceries and set them on the table for Sue to sort and put away.

Seeing it was quite a lot of bags and she did want to use the table for breakfast, she decided to do it now.

She had gone through two bags when she reached into the next and pulled out a folded-up piece of paper. She thought at first it was probably the agent's grocery list but unraveled it just the same to look. Her heart stopped and she almost was unable to stand. Recomposing herself she put the paper into her pocket and went looking for Larry.

She found him where she always does first thing in the morning, sitting on his throne. It was like a ritual with him every day always at the same time.

She just sat down on the edge of the bathtub seeing the toilet was in a small room inside the larger bathroom and waited.

She took the paper out of her pocket and kept rolling it in her hands repeatedly and just staring down at it.

When Prince Charming finally was through and with a smile on his face came from his anointed throne room, he greeted Sue with a big "Good morning, what is for breakfast?"

His smile turned to cold immediately when he saw Sue's face; he reached down and took the paper from her hand, Sue never looking up, just sitting there silently.

Larry opened the paper and read "I have Tami, if you ever think of seeing her alive follow my instructions."

They knew without having to read it who this was from.

Larry fell to his knees and continued to read: "You must somehow get out, I do not care how you do it, just do it. Call this number when you can. Go to a public place that has easy access to the public so you feel safe and call me, I am watching you and will contact you there. If you alert the agents of this, Tami will be dead. Doesn't matter if I am free or behind bars, Tami will die."

Larry and Sue knew they had to do something. Right now, the agents might get suspicious, if they do not get out of the bathroom, after being in here for some time now.

They were right, as Larry swung the door open, an agent was standing outside and asked, "Is everything ok?"

Sue replied with a broken smile and said, "Oh you know, as good as it can be." Walking past the agent into the kitchen asking as she passed if they would like anything to eat, making it seem things as usual.

The day went by, and Larry and Sue grew anxious to get out and had no idea on how to get anywhere without agents crawling all over them.

They were sitting watching a movie. Sue commented that she was going to make some buttered popcorn, and as she rose to stand she had a sharp pain, hesitated and grabbed her stomach. It was the first full kick from the new member of the family, but before she could even joyfully express herself, the agents swarmed her like she was giving birth, asking if she was ok and if they could do anything to help, very concerned.

She said, "Just a kick, nothing to worry about."

Larry had already stood up and so walked to the kitchen to help her prepare the popcorn.

She commented, "Do you believe those guys? All that fuss over a small kick, what the heck they would do if it were really something." She laughed, as the popcorn started to pop.

Larry remarked, "They would call out the National Guard I would bet. What a bunch of..." He stops talking, pauses, then says, "They would react without thinking, doing anything you requested." He stood behind her while she shook the pan as Larry whispered his idea to her. At one point she was focused so intently she stopped shaking the pan and without missing a stroke Larry reached up and put his hand over hers and kept the rhythm shaking the pan, all along speaking ever so softly his idea to get them a shot to get out so they might help Tami.

The next morning Sue filled the coffee pot with water, reached in the fridge for the coffee and on opening, found it to be a little short on grinds for a full pot so she went to the pantry to get a new can. The can was up on the shelf just out of reach, so she grabbed a little one step folding stool like the one everyone has in their kitchen. She positioned it, flipped the first step down into position, stepped up and stretched out to grab the can when she let out a scream, stepped down bending over and went to the floor.

Well, you could imagine everyone's concern and she was quickly surrounded by agents as well as Larry.

She was in complete agony grasping her lower stomach area complaining about sharp pains.

The agents went into a complete panic mode and then Larry took charge. "Guys, we need to get her to a hospital ASAP, and I mean like yesterday."

The agents all looked at each other concerned about taking them out to a public place and Larry again spoke up, "Do you want me to call 911 or do you want to do it? Do it now!"

The agent in charge reached for his phone and called frantically to get an ambulance on its way. All the while Sue laid still just moaning and complaining of the pain.

It seemed like hours, but in a short few minutes, it arrived, and she was off to the hospital, surrounded by agents.

Larry had gone earlier back into their bedroom while waiting for the ambulance to arrive to grab the overnight bag they had prepared to take when Sue would deliver; it had some essentials just in case she may need to stay overnight.

Larry road in the back while two agents crammed their way into a single front seat and four other agents followed in two separate cars.

Once at the hospital, the doctor on call kept everyone out of the room so he could do a thorough examination. Larry was the only one allowed to stay. The agents positioned themselves outside the doors entering the emergency room as well as agents on the outside of the single-story building.

A rush of doctors came and went.

If you have ever experienced this you know how it is, not so much while it is going on, you think everyone is so concerned, with all the attention you are receiving.

But later when you receive all these doctor bills from who you have no clue whatsoever, all the consulting fees, well what we do know about hospitals is that any attending physician can visit a patient whether requested or not, it is part of training, but here is the catch, you get to pay for all this attention and training, great system.

Of course, this was really driving the agents totally crazy, all these strange people, male, female, all dressed in hospital attire, some in street clothes, just looking at the charts, others doing checks on IV drip, and equipment being used.

One such technician, dressed in a light blue outfit, wearing glasses, brought in an ultrasound to use to get some good recordings of the baby's condition.

Things calmed down which gave Sue a chance to shut her eyes for some much-needed sleep; she was exhausted.

Just a few short minutes had gone by when the door slowly opened. It was the ultrasound technician.

He stopped partially in the room and stopped, realizing Sue had fallen asleep. He asked Larry in a very soft tone, "I can come back later when she is awake if you like," slowly backing up.

Larry stood up. "No, come on in, she wanted me to wake her if you came by."

Larry touches her arm, rubbing it slowly to not frighten her; she awakens with a smile seeing Larry. She asks, "What's up?"

"The tech is here with the ultrasound."

She says, "Great," and sits up to get a better view of the screen.

As the technician moves everything into position, but prior to turning the monitor on, he asks, "Do you want to know the sex of your baby? Later in the recording, you will be able to tell."

She looks at Larry, as he moves his head back and forth, leans down and whispers to her, "It doesn't matter the sex now, just that it is doing okay."

Sue tells the technician, "No, we do not want to know the sex."

He starts to show them the video, pointing out the shape of the baby's head, saying how the shape is perfect. Next the arms and hands, counting out all fingers and thumbs, A-Okay.

The technician stops at this point and turns the monitor away so not show them what might reveal the sex.

Sue, still very tired, smiles and tells them, "I am going to just lay back a bit while you get to where you need to be in the recording."

Larry smiles, and with his back to the monitor and technician, watches as Sue falls fast asleep. With the beautiful images she has just seen of her baby, it had to be a great relief to her.

Larry started to turn when he felt the technician's hand on his upper arm, grasping it tightly, more than just a warm kind of a grasp, more like the one your parents did when you knew you were in trouble.

Larry slowly rotates to see why this gesture, looking at his hand on his arm then looking up at his face, past the eyeglasses and into the tech's eyes. Larry knew who it was, Frank.

Frank calmly said, "Larry," in an incredibly soft voice, "I do not want to harm you or Sue. You know what I can do so if I want you, Sue or even Tami dead, there is absolutely nothing you can do to prevent it."

Larry cautious but upset says, "Why all the I-Spy crap, get it over with, you have both of us here, why not now, right here."

He replied, "It is not my way. All my victims never know who, why, or when I hit them. Most think before they die, so this is what an accident feels like. They do not know I have just murdered them. You will be no exception."

"Well then why did you want to meet? We were going to do as your note said, but we thought Sue had fallen and needed help. This was not our plan, if it had been, I would have called you."

Frank said, "First off, I have no idea where Tami is and have never known. I went to her house looking for anything that might lead to you two but all I found was a dumb cat.

"Second, I know Sue is carrying a baby and it is not my thing to kill babies or children. That is sacred," smiling but with those deep black glassy eyes, which sent a cold chill through Larry.

"Oh, so you do have a conscious, you draw the line, so what about me, unless it is a miracle, I am not giving birth."

"Let's stop with the remarks," replies Frank. "I wanted to let you know that if the day ever comes that these moron agents or anyone catches me and I go to trial and you testify against me, even if I go to prison or the chair, you and Sue will be dead within 24 hours after my conviction leaving your baby without a dad or mom. Is that what you want?"

Larry, feeling like he had just been run over by a truck, slowly looked up at Frank and just shook his head from side to side, saying no.

Frank spoke up, "Larry, it looks like your baby is healthier than all of us here, and the doctor will be in shortly to talk to you two." Sue startled by the abrupt talking awoke from her light sleep as Frank left the room taking the ultrasound with him.

Larry told Sue that a technician had an emergency call to take care of, but the doctor should be in shortly.

Larry, being who he was, kept it to himself, a burden he would have to bear for a long time; he knew telling Sue would accomplish nothing so why upset her. He never even told her that he had called Frank when he went to get her overnight bag.

Later that night, Sue asked when he wanted to get their plan in place to call Frank. Larry just told her he did not think it would be a good idea and they needed to wait for another time.

They released her later that day, so they returned to the safe house.

The next day, both were awakened by very excited agents.

After the previous day, they thought this activity was unusual.

After a few minutes, one of the agents, taking a breath before speaking, "Tami is alive and back home. She had returned from a trip in a third world country where she had an accident and hospitalized for quite some time before she could return. She had been in a medically induced coma to help while some minor brain swelling from the accident had receded."

Sue wept with joy to know her sister was safe.

Larry knew then that Frank's warning was indeed a warning not to take lightly.

Frank now had made his point and again turned his attention to the accountant. He had decided to wait until the following Thursday when he was almost certain he would be at the motel. His plan was simple, after the escort would leave, he would enter the room while he slept and kill him in the way only Frank could do, making it look just like an accident.

Thursday came and he waited just down the street and as they have done before, the accountant and his escort arrived.

He sat like a hunter on Safari, waiting very patiently for his prey to reveal itself. Surveying everything around to be sure nothing is out of the normal activities.

Around eleven, the door of the room opened with the escort leading the accountant.

The accountant stopped just outside the door; she turns to him as he hands her an envelope and a partially open bottle of what look like vodka.

She then leaves as the accountant slowly looks around, stumbles a bit, before going back into the room, shutting the door behind him.

Frank knew he had to wait just a bit longer to be sure the intoxicated man would be out cold.

An hour went by, and Frank moved in using a key he had made earlier when he had stayed in that very same room.

He uses the key and before opening glances around to be sure no one is watching. Entering and again glancing around, ever so slowly, he closes the door behind him. Hearing accountant snoring, he knows he is out cold.

He walks slowly around the room looking for anything that looks out of place or suspicious. Walking over next to the bed and bending over, he removes a can from his coat pocket, a spray to be sure he is out, but nothing lethal. Remember, he plans it out to look like an accident.

Just as he went to spray, the whole world came down on him with lights and guns pointing at him, FBI agents coming through companion doors, windows, main doors, yelling, "Stay where you are, hands above your head!"

Before he knew it, he was thrown down, handcuffed, grabbed up by four agents, thrown into a van, and whisked away. It had all been a setup from the get-go, from the accountant to the escort service down to the motel manager. They knew Frank had a contract for the accountant and would take this opportunity and set it all up.

It was now early the next day. Before sunrise, Larry and Sue woke to, again, the rustling of agents in and around the safe house.

They heard a soft tapping at their door. Larry gets up putting on his robe seeing it was a cold morning.

Upon opening, the agent who was knocking steps aside, coming down the hall, a very special friend, Agent Fyfe himself; he had been waiting for months to give them the good news, that day was today. Frank was now in custody.

Sue was overjoyed by the news and could not stop crying and laughing out loud; Larry was less thrilled but knew he had to show some joy to help keep his secret locked up, that he had seen and talked to Frank.

Agent Fyfe came up to Larry and asked, "So this is good news, right?" Looking and smiling at Larry.

Larry responded with a big, subdued yahoo. He then asks, "How long before the trial?"

Fyfe seemed to sense something wrong with Larry, but answered, "I think it should be soon, well as soon as any trial can be, but they have been accumulating evidence all along so my guess they will push it right along."

Larry was now filled with another kind of fear, not like the one he has been feeling since the canyon shooting but one that directly affects him and Sue. He had no idea what to do, tell the agents, Fyfe, who should he tell? He must tell someone, but who can he confide in when his and Sue's life hangs in the balance?

He starts thinking of all possible things that could or might happen. He thought, how can or can Frank really get to him locked up? He believed he had the means and the ways to do just that.

Can he get to them once they have been put into a government protection program? He doubts that but is not sure.

Would he get to them before they went into a program? He could be is his guess, and he would.

Something came to mind about a trial he heard of where the witnesses testified but were in an undisclosed location and did so through a television link. Surely with today's communication systems that could be arranged and would give them the time to get into a program. He thought, could he trace the transmission?

Larry knew at this point he had to consult with someone and then tell Sue of their position with Frank's threat.

But who could he trust with such important information, what if Frank has someone or "The Someone" he contacts in his back pocket.

Except for the one mistake Frank made about the accountant, he has been one step ahead all along and Larry was sure he would not make another.

The pressure and stress level kept rising with every thought and idea Larry could come up with and he still could not decide on what, who, or when to do anything but one thing for sure, time was not on his side. He would soon be forced into deciding and then telling Sue.

5

"THE TRIAL"

The trial came sooner than Larry liked but he had no choice in the matter.

Sue and he went through another whole bombardment of questions that they had to already answer a hundred times before.

Frank had been charged with two premediated murder counts in the first degree.

No one knew of his involvement killing the other unfortunate hiker.

Larry had asked about giving testimony via cable, but the prosecuting attorney felt a public testimony would have a much better effect on the jury.

Larry was not concerned about himself so much as he was for Sue, especially being in the latter stages of her pregnancy.

The defense attorney made numerous appeals to get more time to prepare for trial, but most were declined by the Judge.

First Frank's appearance to the judge to give him his plea, innocent of all charges.

Once the trial started, it took a week or so for the jury selection with Frank's attorney declining almost all jurors for one reason or another.

The judge totally frustrated after yet another long unproductive day of juror potentials, asked to see both attorneys in his chambers.

He told Frank's attorney to stop with all the stalling on jury selection.

He responded back, stalling, "These are Frank's protected rights to a fair trial, a selection of his peers."

Judge responds, "A selection of his peers is not likely. Frank is one of a kind, he has no peers"

The judge firmly replies, "Get on or I will select the jury for you."

He protested but moved on and accepted six out of the next twelve jurors reviewed.

A very gloomy day outside with rain all day, just very fitting considering what has transpired.

The trial started off with plenty of items the judge had to take in consideration before opening statements and the first witnesses to be questioned.

Again, more stalling tactics by the defense.

The opening statements for the most part where short and to the point. Frank's attorney saying they could prove his complete innocents. There was no real evidence connecting him to the killings, no creditable witnesses, and no weapon, seeing Frank disposed the weapon quickly that same day.

The federal attorney calling Frank the devil himself. Claiming they had evidence and a prime witness.

All witnesses and jurors had been sequestered and put up at different locations until testifying.

Many days of testimonies by almost every single person that had anything to do with the least little detail down to the officer who put down the little numbered markers that had some bearing however so insignificant most were. They left no stone unturned to assure Frank could not get out of this one.

Even having their old buddy, the Sheriff having his day in court as well.

His was to state what he knew of Sue and Larry when he met them at the truck stop restaurant.

Frank all along sat quietly next to his attorney, asking questions now and again, sipping on water and seemed completely content in the whole affair going on around him.

Even when pictures of the two men were shown on a large screen, Frank looked almost interested in it like he was seeing it for the first time, jotting down notes as if finely tuning his work so he would be even better the next time a similar task was called upon him once again.

The day Sue would be testifying was coming up fast.

Larry still had not told her about his contact with Frank, he still was not sure if he should even tell her, what difference it would make, would she be totally upset with him for not telling her? Larry was all knotted up inside and about to burst out.

The night before her testimony, they were awarded some very unusual time together and a private outing at a secluded restaurant completely sealed off from anyone else. The waiters were agents and the cooks had been brought in not ever having a clue who they were cooking for or serving.

Larry thought about Frank, going over it back again and again in his mind what is the right thing to do.

Sue broke in and asked, "Honey, what is the matter? You look like you're about to explode. Tomorrow starts the end of our old lives and the beginning of our new; soon we'll be on our own again to start a family. Well I guess we've already done some of that with this one coming soon," glancing down at her extreme size moving into her later months of pregnancy.

With that said, Larry made up his mind, he will take the burden of knowing all on his shoulders and would put his full faith and trust in the program they will be entering soon, The Guardian Angel Program.

He sipped some wine and for the first time in a long time just relaxed. What would happen was beyond his control from now on.

The next day things were extremely tense with the media in full force wanting to get the first real live glimpse of the key witnesses.

Sue was escorted by four FBI agents with many more clearing a pathway in front as well as all sides, covering her with a bulletproof blanket until she had entered the courthouse.

Larry was still tucked away in another safe location; he had no idea what Sue was going through and how long it would be.

Sue was called in by the court and was sworn in; for the first time since that eventful day she got her first one on one look at Frank.

She felt a cold chill run up and down her back as she glanced over time and time again at Frank.

Frank looking back with that blank glassy eyed looked that seems to cut right through you. Not even blinking, just a death type expression.

She had been instructed by the prosecutor not to appear to be looking directly at him, but she found it hard not to look at this person who had changed her life forever.

Before the questioning started, the judge gave a very stern warning that he would not tolerate the least bit of badgering this witness, especially in her condition and fore warned harsh consequences to whoever would try such tactics.

The prosecutions questioning went on and things moved quite rapidly, almost scripted to the point and ended sooner than anyone expected. The prosecutor took heed to the judge's warning for sure.

Turning to the defense's attorney, the judge once again said, "Take heed in my warning in questioning this witness!"

The defense attorney stood up, paused for a moment, poured a glass of water, and sipped from the glass, bent down and asked Frank a question with Frank responding with only a nod and a smile looking directly at Sue.

Something up to now was not something Sue had seen in Frank.

It seemed like hours waiting for him to speak. The judge asked, "Sir, are you ready to ask question this witness?"

"Yes, your honor, we have but one single question for this witness."

He asks, "Can I call you Sue?"

She replied, "That would be okay."

"Sue, did you see Frank shoot the two men?"

Sue hesitated; her expression was one of horror, thinking back to that day. She replies, "When Larry and I saw him standing over the two men with a gun in his hand, Larry took both of us to the ground for protection. Larry made me stay down as he looked up to see Frank shoot the two men."

The defense attorney asks again, "Did you see Frank shoot the two men, yes or no."

"No, I did not see it, only heard the shots."

The defense attorney spoke, "May it please the court, we have no further questions for this witness at this time."

The courtroom exploded with an array of mixed outpouring of excitement and verbal outbursts to the point the judge seemed almost powerless to stop it.

The agents assigned to guard Sue rushed in and surrounded her as she sat in the witness chair in total shock.

Finally, after many attempts and threats to clear the courtroom, the judge regained order and asked the defense attorney if he had heard correctly? He responded with a positive yes, your honor.

The judge told Sue she was released and could step down. As she walked by Frank, looking through the agents surrounding her to get a short glimpse of Frank, he looked and smiled at her.

The media went crazy trying again to get any kind of a statement from Sue, but little did they know that in all the confusion in the courtroom, in the elevator coming down, she had been replaced by a double and Sue was taken out another secured exit back to where Larry was waiting, she thought.

Seeing it took almost the whole day for Sue's testimony and the fact the judge had instructed Sue previously not to discuss her testimony with anyone, which included Larry, it would be the first time the two of them would be alone and away from each other in many days, weeks, and months.

The next morning an armed escort awaited Larry for his day in court like Sue the day previously.

Larry had no idea the masses of people assembled when pulling up to the courthouse steps.

He had not heard what had happened the previous day with Sue, the judge ordered him to total media blackout trying to avoid any effects on his testimony.

As he walked into the courtroom and was sworn in like Sue the day before, Larry too had his first look since his encounter with Frank in the hospital a short while back.

Frank's demeanor was more attentive then with Sue; he had sent out a clear message the day before releasing Sue from what could have been an emotional stressful testimony.

The prosecutor went through his questioning without any hitches and then asked the one question Larry had feared for weeks. "Larry, this is my last question; do you without any question or doubt whatsoever and with your entire mind, soul, and body, witness Frank Mast shoot those two men along that creek that early morning hours?"

Larry looked now directly at Frank. Frank beamed at Larry. Larry hesitated and took a breath still looking directly at Frank. "Yes, Frank Mast is the man I saw shoot those two men by the creek, no doubt whatsoever."

Again, the courtroom exploded, and the judge again took some time to regain order.

The judge looking worn out a bit asked if anyone would like to recess or wait until tomorrow to continue. Both sides declined.

The judge then ordered the defense attorney to commence his questioning.

Larry and Frank still locked in an eye-to-eye battle; even the defense attorney started to ask his first question and stopped to look down at Frank and then to Larry, reaching down for again his glass of water but this time not for show as the day before but to clear his throat knowing there was more here than what appearances made it out to be.

Clearing his voice and finally getting Frank to break away his visual contact, the defense attorney took a track no one had been prepared for. His first question: "Have you had any contact with Frank Mast since the day you supposedly witnessed these shootings?"

Even the prosecution side all sat up; they objected but the judge declined. All the rustling in the courtroom stopped to where you could hear a pin drop. The defense attorney repeated the question, "Have you had any contact with Frank Mast since the day you supposedly witnessed these shootings? Judge, we request you require the witness to answer the question at once."

Larry was in total shock. Frank has set him up from day one, he thought, how could he prove it? He might have a recording; it will make everyone involved, all the agents, look very incompetent and make Larry look like an accomplice to the Frank.

Frank could be playing a hand he does not have, but what if he does? It would be all over.

The judge and attorney now getting frustrated with Larry's lack of answering when the prosecutor made a motion to recess. Larry was obviously under extreme emotional stress and needs some time.

The judge agrees and the court takes a 30-minute recess.

Larry glances over at Frank as he is escorted out. Frank smiles then winks at Larry.

Larry is quickly rushed off into a room in the courthouse where the group of attorneys has assembled to rehash the question, the single question he had been asked in court.

"Have you been in contact with Frank?" one attorney asked in a barking tone.

Larry sat up and answered, "Yes."

"Do you know what you have done?" yelled one attorney. "Why didn't you tell us this before? What were you thinking?"

One of the more prominent attorneys, Rob, calmly walked over to Larry, pulled him off to the side and asked what his contact had been, all along the other attorneys grouped together trying to come up with some kind of strategy. Every so often shouting a question or comment at Larry.

Larry told Rob the why, where, and what went down with Frank at the hospital.

Rob asked Larry if he needed anything and then turned to the others and said, "Gentlemen, after calmly discussing this situation with Larry I feel we can counter with Larry being under all the stress and pressure and also the threat of harm to his family from Frank. The jury will understand, they will not understand any one of you seeming to be alarmed or totally in the dark about this, even though we may be. We need to appear fully informed, calm and cool about the whole thing. Do I make myself clear?

"We must go back into the courtroom unified as a team to bring justice to this terrible crime Frank Mast has committed. We cannot let him manipulate this court or jury in his favor. Are we all in agreement?"

· "Yes."

One by one they all agreed.

They asked Larry, in a much calmer tone, to explain the events surrounding his contact with Frank.

Larry explained that day at the hospital in detail.

Some were hoping the judge would not reconvene but dismiss everyone for the day.

Again, Rob stepped forward. "Gentlemen," calmly speaking, "we want to go back into that courtroom now and get on with this even if it is only for a few moments to rebut some of the negativity surrounding the previous events of the day."

He pointed at one of the attorneys and instructed him to get in touch with the court and see when they could reconvene the proceedings.

Larry, sitting off by himself quietly sipping a bottle of water, looked almost in a state of shock. Who would not under these circumstances, he thought.

Rob noticed this and approached Larry sitting down next to him grabbing a bottle of water from the center of the table, and opening it up, he takes a long drink, sighs and he asks Larry, "How you holding up?"

Larry openly apologizes to Rob about not telling him about his contact with Frank.

"Look here, no one can fault you about keeping that to yourself. You have heard terrible things over these past months about Frank and what he can do, so it is totally understandable," taking another long drink.

Larry asks, "Rob, pardon my stupid question, but just who the heck are you? I know you are an attorney but when you talk these other attorneys stop and listen, so who are you?"

Rob takes another drink. "Well let me say this one thing that might make sense, I am their boss and my boss lives in the White House. Yes, sir, my boss is the President of the United States.

"I answer only to him and him alone; I am special counsel to the White House in all matters that have repercussions to the security of the United States and the President has been following this all along and told me to take this matter as if it was a threat, a threat that a young American couple could be put through such hell and still stand up to all the turmoil that they have been put through need some special help."

Larry sits back and smiles a slight smile and says chuckling, "I wish I had voted for him!"

They all return to the courtroom; I should add a packed courtroom and Larry resumes his seat for questioning.

He is calmer now that his well-kept secret is now off his shoulders but still unsure how it will all play out.

Again, the defense attorney for Frank comes forward and asks, "Have you had any contact with Frank Mast since the day you supposedly witnessed the shootings?"

Without hesitation and in a clear loud voice Larry replies, "Yes, I have."

The courtroom explodes with reporters running out to get the first scoop out on this newly found information.

The judge regains order and ask the attorney to proceed with his questioning and he continues questioning on their contact.

Larry states, "At the hospital when we had to take Sue there for stomach pains, after we thought she fell in the kitchen."

The attorney hesitated then realized the chance of Frank pressuring Larry.

He was ever so careful not to ask a question or leave an opening for Larry to tell them about the threat to himself and Sue Frank had made in the hospital.

All this time Frank has his almost glass appearing eyes focused on Larry, not even blinking, hunters' eyes, that look right through you.

The defense attorney continues with questions on the actual day Larry supposedly saw the shooting, bypassing any further questions on the hospital.

Larry is asked the distance he was from the actual scene, if he wore glasses, had a hearing problem of any kind, questions that may raise any kind of reasonable doubt in the juror's mind. Larry stood fast and answered them with clear and clean responses leaving no doubt whatsoever.

"One last question if I may, how could you know if the men were alive at the time of the shooting you said took place?"

Larry stops to think it through. "I cannot say to that at all, sir. What I saw was that man," pointing at Frank, "shoot each man in the head."

Defense attorney says, "No further questions."

The prosecutions sees an advantage that the defense has not wanted to come out, the contact at the hospital. So, they ask the court.

"Judge, we have one question to ask of this witness if we could please."

The judge replied, "Go right ahead."

"Larry, did Frank make any direct threats to you or anyone else when you had contact with him at the hospital?"

Looking at Frank directly he says, "Yes, he said no matter what happens to him, if I testified against him, he would kill Sue, Tami and myself even if he is locked up."

The attorney thanks him and tells the judge that is all.

The judge asks the defense if they have any further questions; they answer no thank you.

Questioning over and Larry was asked to step down.

He was free to go, no more questions and the next day the final statements by both sides were heard and the juror sent back to deliberate and bring back a verdict.

Within 48 hours they brought back two guilty counts for murder in the first degree.

Now Larry and Sue, being reunited right after Larry's time on the witness stand, were rushed away under as you might guess some very tight security.

An enclosed van with no windows in the back for obvious reasons not to see in but it did strike them funny that they also could not see out.

When the van stopped, the side door slid open, and they were inside what appeared to be a hangar with a small jet with its engines already running awaiting for them.

They did stop and said their goodbyes to all the agents, and as they made their way towards the plane, at the bottom of the steps was Agent Fyfe.

He greeted both with open arms and heart. He said, "We had some very bumpy moments the past months, but you always stood strong." A tear rolled down his cheek. He wished them all the best in the future and once again thanked them for everything they had done, slightly patting Sue on the tummy and saying, "Take care of this little one."

They boarded the plane, and the door was shut behind them.

They did not even have a chance to sit down, and the plane started to move so they hurriedly strapped in and held hands.

For the first time in a long time, they felt at ease and peace within.

As the plane taxied down the runway, Sue remembered the days gone by and all the people they met throughout the ordeal they had been through.

As the plane stopped, then started its rollout down for takeoff, Sue slides the window cover up but found the window completely blacked out.

She slides down the window cover, as her past life was over and a new one was just beginning.

What could possibly be worse than what they had just been put through.

"THE GUARDIAN ANGEL PROGRAM"

The plane ride was amazingly comfortable, and an exceptionally large spread of drinks and food had been laid out for them to enjoy.

While taking a break and enjoying some beverages furnished on the plane, Larry said, "I am going to go talk to the pilot to see how long they would be flying," but as he tried to open the door, it was locked and a small plaque read, 'No Entering of Unauthorized Personnel', again kind of weird but he understood with all the terrorist threats and high airport security it was the way it is.

Sue had been allowed to call and talk with her sister Tami and was prepared for never being able to see her sister again, another sad but absolute fact of their new life.

Tami herself was going into a witness program, not that she knew anything, but the authorities thought it best for her own protection.

After quite some time they landed and again when exiting the plane, found themselves inside a hangar with a car waiting to pick them up, no one else around.

They got into the car which, like most transportation, was completely without a view to the outside.

They arrived and was let out inside a badly lit garage, a small light above a single door.

Larry and Sue walked through the first set of doors followed by multiple sets of doors, arriving in what might be a lobby of a very up scaled hotel, not what they were expecting at all.

They approached what looked like a front desk.

Two computer monitors with a picture of Larry on one and Sue on the other.

The instructions for them, press the key to the last letter of the name appearing on the screen.

Instruction will follow, please be specific in answering all questions.

First instruction, your full and complete name.

Once your full name is inputted, you will receive additional instructions and a key.

The instructions will appear on the screen which say, you will receive a room key, it comes up through a door in the countertop in front of the monitor screen.

Instructions to proceed to their room number on the key where they would receive further information concerning their future.

Before doing this, Larry, thinking they would be going to the same room, wanting to have some fun, told Sue, "Look, I bet we are going to find out what our new names and where we will be living so let's not tell each other until we have both read everything they are about to give us. Okay?"

Sue excited agrees and puts her name in, sure enough out pops a key with on screen instructions to its location and Larry following up doing the same and of course, receiving the same information.

They are startled when an elevator door opens.

At first, they hesitate, but they enter the elevator and to their surprise, two screens, one with Sue and one with Larry's names on the screens. They have been instructed to different floors, kind of strange but what they have been through is a welcome change.

"Ok, let us go to our rooms, get our stuff, and meet back down in the lobby to see what lays ahead," Larry says. "You up for that?"

"Sure, it should only be a couple of minutes," she replies. "Any way I must use the bathroom, I'm about to burst!"

They both go to their rooms, use the keys to enter and inside sitting on a table is a large envelope. On the envelope it reads, "Do Not Open Until Instructed To."

Sue of course heads for the ladies' room and as she comes out grabs the packet and heads to the elevator.

Larry being on another floor takes some time to wash his face and heads to the elevator as well.

Too much surprise to them both, the elevator they used to go to their floors cannot be accessed back from the floors they are on, no buttons to push.

Larry being a contractor is really puzzled but sees at the end of the corridor another elevator and to the side a white lit button.

Relieved but still confused, he walks over, pushes the button and the door opens. He walks in and without even pushing anything else, the door shuts and takes off, dropping like a rock, but slowing down and stopping.

Larry just cannot wait to see Sue and tell her of his new name, but when the door opens no Sue, just a black car with dark windows and the back rear door open.

Larry says out loud, "Man, don't you guys have any other color but black."

With no response from anyone, not even Sue.

She has to be in the car waiting so he walks over and no Sue, strange, all the glass is darkened out and there is a glass partition between the front seat and back, so he walks around to the driver's side to ask the driver if he has seen Sue but the door is locked and even after pounding on the door and glass, no response from the driver. The windshield is even so dark you cannot see in, one way glass.

Larry waits what seems like hours hoping any minute now Sue will be popping out of the elevator, but no Sue and the only way out is in the back seat of this car.

Larry thinks to himself, maybe she has already left, and she is at the new house waiting for him, maybe.

So, he decides the next best move would be to get in the car and let it take him to her.

He sits down and closes the door, the doors lock, engine starts, and off he goes.

He does notice that there are no door handles and locks on the inside of the doors, something he wishes he had noticed before he got in the damn thing.

While traveling for a few minutes, a recording comes over the speaker system. "Welcome to the Guardian Angel Project, please open the envelope and read the instructions inside."

Nothing else to do so why not.

He opens it and inside is a social security number, driver's license, birth certificate, bank account, description of his new job, a home address, keys to car, much, much more and your new name is Greg Moore.

Larry is still worried about Sue and that she is probably totally going crazy about now when the car stops, and the door opens.

He steps out and sure enough it is in front of a house in a nice neighborhood.

He takes one step away from the car and it takes off.

Larry runs up to the door and to his surprise it is locked so he grabs his keys from his envelope and opens the door yelling out, "Sue!" but she is nowhere to be found.

Now panic starts to set in—who can I call to find out what has happened to Sue? He cannot just call anyone, no one is going to believe him. Call Fyfe.

He will know what's going on for sure, now what was that number, oh yea. He runs to the phone hanging on the wall, good dial tone, dials up Fyfe's number and it is a recording. "You have reached Agent Fyfe. I will be out of town and contact while traveling out of the country, leave a message and I will call you back upon my return."

He wanders around a bit and goes to the refrigerator and finds it completely stocked up with a week's worth of food, same with the large pantry but double the amount of food and supplies.

Checking out the rest of the house, he finds everything he could possibly need and then some, as if he had lived here for years.

So, he opens the door leading from the house to the garage, to his surprise, a brand-new truck completely optioned out.

What could have happened?

Where is Sue and what can I do to find her?

7

"THE SEARCH"

Exhaustion takes over, and as Larry leans back on the couch, he falls into a deep sleep.

Waking up the next morning, he prepares himself for what may be the most trying days of his life to come.

He walks out the front door and to his surprise finds a daily paper on the front step, reaches down, picks it up and opens it up to read about Frank Mast's conviction.

A chill ran through him knowing he now has two things to fear, not finding Sue and Frank having him killed.

He must find Sue first so he can protect her, his first and foremost thought, giving him the energy to get up and get going.

He heads back into the house and grabs the envelope; he scavenges through it looking for a bank book, opens it, flips pages, to his surprise, sees a deposit of $ 250,000!!

He then gets the information about his job; it appears he is in sales, but the name does not reference to anything he recognizes.

Ok, money in the bank, a brand-new truck to drive, and all the time in the world to hunt for Sue.

He continues to think, she is not in any type of danger, she is probably sitting in the wrong house at a different location thinking I will pop in at any minute, yes, keep that positive thought going, she's fine, I just must find her.

One thing for sure, we are both in the same city or at least within a drive from our drop location so get a map and do some planning, what map and for what city, I don't have a clue where I am!

The newspaper dummy, it will have a city and state reference. He grabs up the paper and reads in small print, 'Casa Grande, Arizona.' Thinking that's OK, a small town but then realizing that within 75 miles are two of the largest cities in the United States, Phoenix and Tucson and those cities are surrounded by multiple smaller cities that make his location look small in comparison. It is not going to be an easy task, not one bit of evidence to start with and millions of people to talk to.

How does one start such a task? Well, like his pappy use to say, you start a long journey one step at a time.

So, in this case he thought maybe the first step would be to take one step back and trace back to the point when they had been together, maybe a small clue on how they got separated or the reason why they got separated.

The last time he was with Sue was in the elevator; it stopped on Sue's floor, and she got off and I watched her put her key into the door as the elevator door closed to take me to my floor.

Go back, go back even further than that, the lobby, and the computer. What was different besides it not having a human soul around and just that crazy computer, heartwarming I should add.

It asks for us to put in our names separately and we did. I went first putting in mine, Larry J. Williams, then waited for my information then Sue went next entering Sue L. Johnson. Her information popped up, so nothing there. What was the reason for the mix up? He thinks hard, before that the car ride and plane trip but nothing that could get screwed up, or was there.

He sat down in the family room and reached for the TV remote and switched it on. All the time pondering over and over the steps they had taken and what might have been done wrong, there had to be something.

It was late and Larry had spent all day trying to come up with some answers but struck out at every swing he took.

He went into the kitchen to warm up a small dinner and sit down in front of the TV to eat. The evening news had just come on and the headlines seemed insignificant to what he was going through right now.

He was about done with his meal and reach over to shut the TV off when a report about some identity theft came on, identity theft using a computer.

It caught his attention, so he paused to watch and listen. It was a report on how easy it was for someone to steal your identity and how to avoid becoming a victim.

It said to be sure to only give correct information when dealing with computers, never give out your passwords and keep all personal information to a minimal never giving out your address, and bank account numbers.

Computers only know what they receive, junk in, junk out. It is not the computer that robs you but the person using the information so be incredibly careful.

Larry turned off the TV but something about this last report stuck with him. He couldn't get it off his mind to the point he just sat back down on the couch and again kept running the past few days over and over again and again but this time he kept coming back to the computer in the lobby. What was it that they did that got them separated? It all started at the moment after they entered their names.

It was around four A.M. when he got up off the couch and made his way into the bedroom, brushed his teeth, washed his face, changed into some night clothes, and laid down in bed.

His heart was really turning over at this point not having Sue next to him. He said out loud, Sue, "I wish you well wherever you are, I love you, I love our new baby, and my only regret is not having married you all these years."

Larry had a cold chill come over him, marry Sue, we were not married, and she entered her name as she should have.

Fyfe told us the Guardian Angel Project was the most newly formed secretive program ever, that individuals can live out their lives in total peace and fulfillment.

Individuals! Not couples that had been together. Junk in, junk out says the computer.

Sue had been given a totally different identity than me, a computer glitch in a new system that may not have been set up for couples but individuals, which had to be the connection, it must be what has happened.

So, what now? Well for one thing, he knew Sue was one hundred percent safe and secure, both Sue and the baby. Larry smiled thinking of the little one who could be coming any day, he would be a father and man was he looking forward to that.

For a moment he felt sad but then once again he knew he would find his family if it took a lifetime to do.

Now that he had figured out the glitch, he needed to come up with a plan to find Sue.

Run some newspaper ads, could not do that, everyone would know including the bad guys and surely, they would be dead.

Hire a private detective, could not and should not trust anyone at this point.

Go back and get in touch with some of the agents, cannot do that either, would expose us and put them all in harm's way.

There must be a way, a safe way to look but not be detected.

Well one thing for sure, he had a long wait until Fyfe returned so he had that as an option to fall back on so he figured he would spend the month just looking.

He started out looking at all the hospitals in the area including Phoenix and Tucson, looking for newly born children. This was the obvious place to start seeing she had to be just days away from delivering.

He had hope she would stay with the boy and girl's name they had picked out, a boy, either Drake or Deven, and if a girl, Tana, Lilly, or Elizabeth.

So, he checked every day for newborn children using those names. Weeks went by and no luck.

Time moved on and now it would be long past Sue's delivery date; the names had to pop up soon, but the next following weeks, no luck.

It could be any day Fyfe could return and Larry was getting anxious to get some outside help from anywhere he could, but he knew any help from someone in the past would be jeopardizing their life and his, something not to be taken lightly.

He was hoping Fyfe would return his call and the idea of him coming to help was totally out of the question, but he was hoping anyway.

So, onto the task at hand, checking and rechecking every hospital day in and day out, going through every newspaper he could get his hands on and checking every newborn name hoping to see the one is they had picked out.

That day did come, a Drake T. Smith, born outside of Phoenix in the small town of Apache Junction, does not list a father's name, no siblings, no closest relatives, might it be Sue?

He checks out the date of birth, which was just two days ago, man that would be a small miracle. He knew time was running out so he runs to the phone, makes a quick phone call to the hospital. "May I have the maternity ward please?" he asks.

"One moment," a nurse answers.

"Maternity ward, may I help you please?"

"Yes, thank you," Larry says very nervously. "Can you tell me if Sue Smith and her new baby boy is still there?"

Silence, then the nurse asks, "Are you family?"

Larry pauses, thinks to himself, I must be incredibly careful here, it is obvious the nurse is well trained not to give out info over the phone and the newspaper did not list any family members. He replies, "Just a friend of the family."

He hears her rustling papers, "Yes, both her and the baby are here, but scheduled to check out as soon as the doctor signs the release forms."

Larry is busting a gut with excitement. "Can you put me through to her room please?"

"Yes, that is possible, hang on one moment." She comes back on the phone, "I'm sorry, she is not in her room right now, let's see, she isn't scheduled for any test that I can see, she must be walking around right at this moment or may be down in the cafeteria. Can I take a message and get it to her?"

Now Larry is way past waiting. "Can you give me some directions please and I will drive on over and surprise her?"

She willingly gives Larry directions and tells him from where he is it would be about a thirty-to-forty-five-minute drive.

Man, oh man you would have thought Larry was trying out for the Indianapolis 500, thirty minutes at normal speed, ten minutes at Larry's speed, all the while just smiling and with such anticipation to be with Sue and his new baby boy, just imagine the feelings he was going through!

Larry arrives at the hospital and is out the car door before it stops, runs into the main lobby, slides up to the information desk.

"Sir, you must be a new daddy looking for the maternity ward," smiling and asking does the receptionist.

To Larry, out of breath, she says, "Third floor, sir, elevators down and to the right."

"Thanks!"

Larry now with sweat running down his forehead helps the elevator doors open as he arrives on the third floor. He runs past room after room glancing to see if he catches Sue out of the corner of his eye and slams right into a, let us say, a very big-boned nurse.

Larry knocked to the floor and this nurse bearing down over him, annoyed more by the fact he ran into her, she says, "Sir, you know you are not supposed to be running in here. Is there a fire somewhere?" She smiles looking down at Larry.

"I am looking for Sue Smith, she had a baby boy here a couple days ago and I was told she was still here, is she?"

"Well, she and the baby were just released fifteen minutes ago and headed down the elevator."

"Was she alone? "

"No sir, she was carrying a baby for goodness sakes, you must be the daddy I suppose."

"No just a friend of the family here to help her out."

"Well get yourself going then and help that poor girl out, you can probably catch her down in the parking garage. I helped her to the elevator and asked her what level and she said the garage level so get on with it," again smiling and this time laughing out loud. "My goodness, thank God women have the babies."

Larry thanked her for all her help and headed down the elevator, garage level.

The doors opened and there was a dead silence; he stopped to listen for anything that might help him get direction to where Sue was parked.

What was a few seconds seemed like minutes and still nothing, no engine noises, no talking, no sound of someone walking, nothing. He was too late, she had already left.

Larry's joy turned to heartache. Head hung low, he headed back over to the elevator doors but did not have the strength to push the button. He just fell to his knees, turned, and leaned back against the doors, frustration and total exhaustion fell over him.

Then a noise he did not recognize, there it is again, what is that noise, again ever so faintly he heard it again, by God that is a baby crying!

He jumps to his feet and runs in the direction of the sound; it gets louder, looking down the long aisles running by, crying getting louder. He rounds a corner, there, standing by a car, a woman putting a baby in a car seat.

How do I approach her? He walks ever so slowly, gets within twenty feet or so and says, "Sue, is that you?"

She answers, "Yes, it is" and comes up out of the car, turns towards Larry, their eyes lock onto each other. "Can I help you?" she asks.

Larry stops in his tracks; it's not his Sue.

"I am sorry," he says, "I also have a girlfriend named Sue who is having a baby and I thought it was you, please forgive me."

She must have noticed how Larry looked completely defeated and lost.

She walks slowly over to Larry and gives him a hug. "Do you want to see Drake my new baby boy?"

Larry at first started to shake his head no, then says, "Sure, I need a pick me up."

He walks around to the open door and sleeping ever so peacefully is this baby all wrapped up in a wraparound blanket with only his face visible.

Emotions got the better of Larry at this time. He broke down as tears filled his eyes and rolls down his cheeks. She hugs him from behind and asks, "Is there a problem?"

"No, no problem, I must go now and find my Sue." He starts to walk away then stops and asks, "If you wouldn't mind telling me, why did you name your baby Drake?"

"Sure, it was my father's name."

"Oh, that's nice, well good luck to you and little Drake."

She says, "You'll find your Sue real soon."

Larry notices a tear running down her cheek.

Larry now starts walking out of the garage to his car parked who knows where but walk he does, taking every step one at a time, just like his pappy told him to do.

The next day brings no more than all the previous days before, more searching with no more getting close to finding her.

Days, then weeks, that turn into months.

One day he decided to switch things up once he realized if Sue has had the baby by now and that if she was overdue would some kind of a record, not going to happen these days.

His cell phone rings and a somewhat familiar voice was on the other end.

Larry whispers, "Fyfe, is this you?"

Seconds go by and no reply, but Larry knows someone is still there. Again he asks, "Agent Fyfe?"

Again, no reply but there is someone listening, he senses it.

Larry stops, thinks, oh my god could it be Frank?

Now fear runs rampant as he is not sure if calling Fyfe was a good idea. Why did I do that? I put everyone at risk.

Not sure what to do, he says, in a loud responsive way, "Oh I am sorry, you must have the wrong number, you might try and dial the number again to be sure you did it correctly, sorry," and hung up.

Now if it was Frank, he knew he was in big trouble and started to figure out what he should do, where to go and pull him away from everyone to protect them all.

He decides to get out of Arizona as fast as he can and put as much distance between himself and this place right now.

He grabs up as much as he could, shoves it into a duffle bag, snatches up a few items from the fridge, throws it all into the truck, which is parked inside the garage, runs around to the driver's side, starts it up, hits the garage door opener and watches as the door opens anticipating backing up and getting out of here quickly.

In his haste to get his stuff in, a bottle of water fell, wedged itself under the throttle pedal, so he reaches down to free it up, lifts, looks out the mirror and there standing at the end of the car is a figure of a man.

Larry's heart stops, Frank!

He is frozen in time and cannot do anything but hope whatever he is about to do to him he does it quickly and mercifully.

The man approaches and Larry closes his eyes.

A knock on the car door window but Larry is too frightened to even look up.

Then he hears, "Larry, hey Larry, are you all, right?"

Larry slowly raises his head and opens his eyes. "Agent Fyfe, what the hell are you doing here?"

He gets out and gives Fyfe a bear hug and lifts him off the ground.

Fyfe says, "Let us go inside where we have more privacy."

Larry cannot shut up, finally after all this time a face and someone he can talk to. Relief and joy flush over Larry.

"How did you find me?" he asks.

"Well to tell you the truth, I could lose my job over this but when you called a while back, I had a trace put on your cell phone and located you and have been watching you for some time now and I had to be sure you were alone. I was in the car garage when you met that nice girl and her baby, man that was hard to take. Have you had any luck in finding Sue?"

Larry spent the next few hours telling Fyfe all the details.

"Man, I thought the Guardian Angel Project was our answer to get more folks like you and Sue to come forward to help us out, but after this screw up, not so sure anymore, plus how the heck am I supposed to tell them about this glitch if I'm not even supposed to be here."

Larry feeling bad, "Man I am sorry, but I had no one or no were to turn to, knowing Frank's persistence I could not just call on anyone, you know."

"No, no, that is ok, we will figure something out, but first we need to get you and Sue back together, but how do we do that?"

They move Fyfe's car into the garage, and he brings his bags into the house where Larry directs him to the second bedroom.

That night Larry cooked up a good steak for them both with all the fixings to go with it as well.

They spend the night talking about the past and all Larry has been doing to try and find Sue.

Larry says in a somber voice, "My hope of finding Sue before she has the baby has passed by now and as time goes by so does my hope of ever seeing Sue again."

"Bull," says Fyfe in a boastful manner, "we will find her and your baby, even if we must go to Washington headquarters to get answers, it is obvious that the system has failed and someone has to take the fall for it. The problem is that someone, may not want anyone to know, about the problem and may do something drastic to keep it covered up, maybe not.

"So, we have no idea she is here or even within a hundred miles of here, what her name is, if she has had the baby, if she is looking for you, let's see can we pile anymore on top of this heap?"

Looking at Larry and slightly grinning, Larry also gives up a smirk and both, trying desperately to release some of that internal stress.

The next morning brings another day of hope but as the days go by hope is replaced with an urgency and desperation to find her.

Fyfe has not much time left before returning to his duties but vows to spend every moment he has helping.

He has no options to play now accept to try and contact someone close to the Guardian Angel Project or who he thinks might get him closer to the Project person that might can help.

He makes a call to his office asking, "Who is our contact for getting someone into the Guardian Angel Project?"

The reply is not one he was looking for: "Once we have someone who needs protection, then the level of protection is decided by someone outside this office, and we are then contacted by them not us contacting them."

"Strange, so who? We never get a name just when the time happens for them to enter the Project, we get instructions via email when the vehicle will arrive to pick them up."

Fyfe asks with some hesitation, "So like with Larry and Sue with Frank Mast's case, the day the car came for them, a vehicle arrived and from that point we had no contact with anyone."

"That is true, sir, but why ask about this now?"

Lying through his teeth, "I have another case that may warrant the Guardian Angel Project Protection with another couple and just was wondering if I needed to start some paperwork, but you have explained it so thoroughly that through normal channels it will happen if warranted, thanks for the help."

Something must be missing; Fyfe ponders over and over in his mind.

"So, when we request protection and the paperwork is filed someone to forward that info onto someone then another and so on until reaching the right someone who makes that decision, cannot be local has to be at the most top secure position to keep such a thing secure. So many channels that it would be almost impossible to trace, and I am sure some where a paper trail wall blocking us from getting past a certain point."

Fyfe, now after spending all his saved-up time off, must leave Larry on his own, he reassures Larry that even though he is away that he will spend every extra moment looking for Sue.

Larry responds, "Man, if only she would have the same thought. I had to contact you like I did but Sue isn't good remembering numbers, so I am sure it hasn't crossed her mind to even try."

Larry shakes Fyfe's hand and a hug thanking him knowing what risks he has taking trying to help.

Larry now back on his own knows he needs to get somewhat of a life for himself and the reality that he may never be reunited with Sue any day soon.

Weeks, months now pass by Larry staying in the local area hoping to catch a clue with no positive results.

Depression sets in which can be understandable in this circumstance.

"MOVING ON"

Seeing his money was slowly running low and only knowing construction business, he takes a job being a project manager for a large construction company.

This way he could make some money and have most weekends and nights to keep searching.

Many times, over time, he thought he was getting close with no results.

Fyfe calls with leads but all those have failed as well to amount to anything but more desperation.

One day his boss asks Larry to run a project which must be turned around quickly and to sweeten the pot is offered a huge bonus and a full month off when completed.

Man, what an opportunity this could be.

The project is still within an hour of his home so he could commute every day which was very convenient considering his situation.

The project was converting an old run-down building into a new Charter School and had less than one hundred eighty days to complete.

At first the project went along smoothly.

Typical issues with sub-contractors, architects, engineers, and owners. All trying their best to get problems solved, which at times was like putting ten pounds of food in a one-pound freezer bag. Never an easy task, but usually ends up getting done.

The days to complete the job starting to run out, Larry had to spend every minute he had, seven days a week trying to finish up. Twenty-one days to the finish line that needs forty-eight days.

He just kept thinking as he has done now for months. He knew the outcome would be a whole month looking for Sue and what now would be a two or three-year-old son or daughter, so he kept up the frantic pace and pushed all his sub-contractors to the bone to finish up on or before the deadline.

Larry helped the school by getting portions done ahead of schedule and worked with the inspectors to allow them to occupy these spaces, this way they could get ready when students can get started to school.

They could move in desks, shelving, supplies, and other like items.

Teachers were allowed in but until it had been passed off by the authorities, no students allowed.

He had two weeks to get a final inspection and the C of O; Certificate of Occupancy, then he was off for a month.

The next two weeks were the worst two weeks of the entire project, if it could go wrong, it did.

Biggest issues, waiting on back ordered items. Every sub-contractor had something that either been missed or changed and had to be re-ordered.

Larry knew he had the best of the best in his crews and subs from the first day of the start of the project.

With days to spare, all back ordered items had come in and where being installed.

Then disaster hit.

Everything seemed to come crashing down. The biggest problem, a main water line breakage, shutting water down to the entire school.

So now you have five hundred kids and faculty without running water and the quickest it can be dug out, repaired, or replaced, will be at least three days, not good at all.

The school would lose thousands of dollars not opening on time with the kids not attending classes. The kids losing out on days that would have to be made up somehow through the school season.

Larry makes some calls to the city inspectors to tell them of the situation.

Somehow, they need to figure out a reasonable solution to this problem.

Larry asks one, "Do we need to at least get gold tag?"

A gold tag is a tag of temporary C of O and usually give a time that any life-threatening issues have been completed one hundred percent.

The issue, what would it take to get the water back on.

He stops to think, then asks, if we can get the water turned on from a positive source, could we get a Gold Tag with enough time to dig up the break, order the materials to repair, and turn the water on?

The city officials replied with a definite yes, would be to our best interest as well.

Larry considers running a hose to a fire hydrant but after further investigation and with this being such an old building in an out of the way location, the nearest hydrant is a long way off.

He then looks at hooking up the water truck to the building but when he realizes that the water must be potable, which means consumable to humans, the condition of water truck tank, knowing kids may drink this water, nixes that idea.

He then comes up with a plan; he needs a big tank, but it needs to be clean and sanitized for consumption, so it hits him, contact the local dairy company, bring in a tanker truck and instead of milk fill the tanker with water, hookup to the main line inside the school property with a pump and this tanker.

Let's take a moment to see why Larry came up this idea, and a little bit of insight to milk companies. Larry at one time had a project at a dairy facility.

While there, he received a complete run down of the site.

Dairies are like little inner cities for milk cows. They have housing, a complete hospital, sewage, and reclamation department to mention just a few.

The dairy cows live almost like on open range, meaning the cows only have gates that keep them separated for certain reasons.

Safety for the younger ones, sick, mamas, and bulls.

But for the most part, they come and go as they please.

Example, when he first arrived on site for a job walk, he stopped at a gate house building that had an electric gate and cattleguard installed, this keeps them from leaving the area, very large area.

Driving into the facility which had to be hundreds, possibly thousands of acres, he noticed most of the gates were open, with cows walking around like they own the place.

When he stopped at the largest barn. He noticed a line of cows coming out of the building, no fencing, no one watching, just a long line of cows.

He was met by a representative of the facility, Jim.

Larry first commented, "Do you guys know you have gates open and cows walking around?"

Jim laughed. "Yes sir, you see, well let's go inside and I can fill you in," still laughing from Larry's comment.

Once inside, Larry couldn't believe what he saw, cows walking in and out with no one guiding them and again no restrictions whatsoever.

Jim seeing Larry's expression says, "Let's go up into the observation area and it will all start to make sense from there."

They walked up a flight of stairs leading to a room that was mostly glass and a door leading to a catwalk, which led to every area below in this huge barn.

Jim first explained, "The cows all know how, where, and when they are supposed to be twice a day for milking. You see, they like to be milked. How would you like to be carrying around all that milk," smiling.

"First thing to understand, this goes on 24 hours a day, 365 days a year, year after year. They come from the pastures on their own and enter the building where they go to the wash areas to be washed. Then they go to the milk stations to be attached to the automated milking machines to collect the raw milk. After, they leave and go back to their designated pastures to eat and relax to wait for the next milking."

Larry is completely mystified by all this. Jim asks, "What you think so far?"

"This is quite incredible; never had any idea this was going on."

Jim, replies, "There is a lot more. Let's go."

They both go downstairs, but before they go through a door, Jim stops and turns to Larry. "We are entering the vacuum pump room. This is the equipment room drawing the milk from the cows."

They enter the room; the noise level is intense so Jim motions Larry to follow, only spending a few seconds in the room.

Once out of the room, door shut, and noise behind them, Jim says, "If you were to stay in that room any longer than we were, you would need ear protection."

Jim walks a few steps, stops just outside the room to talk.

"You see, from the minute the cows are attached to the milking machines, through the pasteurization of the milk, to trucking, and packaging, the milk is never exposed to the outside elements until it reaches the open milk carton in your house."

Jim and Larry head out to a smaller building. On entering, Jim tells Larry, "This is our hospital equipped with a complete maternity ward, surgery, and well care center."

Walking through and outside of the building, Jim points out a huge mountain of, well, cow manure.

That mountain is used after it is processed to fertilize the grounds that grow the alfalfa and other crops needed to feed all the animals.

What is not used is sold off to companies needing raw materials for fertilizers.

Next, Jim points out an area which from the odor in the air, is obvious, a sewer plant to recycle water.

Jim stops and waits a few seconds. "So Larry, we use very little offsite materials, we recycle many of the resources that we use, in many ways, to try and be as efficient as we can be."

This ended the tour, so the two went off for the reason Larry was there, a small project at one of the barns.

Larry was successful in the bidding of this project and has many times over the years continued working for the dairy.

Larry always loved watching how just glass of milk is only a small portion of the equation. But his true reason was watching the cows doing their part.

This all being said, this is why Larry thought of the dairy trucks, sanitized tanks for transporting milk.

He makes the call to the city to give them his idea on the dairy tankers.

After just a few minutes and another short conference call with a few officials, Larry got the nod of approval.

Larry, knowing who he can contact for the trucks, calls his buddies at the dairy farm, and gets the ball rolling.

Seeing one thing in his favor, thank goodness the water broke on a Thursday afternoon just before the weekend. This gives him the weekend to get his plan moving forward.

Larry gets all the players in place, tankers not just one tanker but two, full of good clean water.

Contacting all the sub-contractors, not just the one who would be doing the repairs, but all major subs, explaining the situation, needing any help in many aspects of this major undertaking.

Crews that had nothing to do with water or even plumbing pitched in to help.

To Larry's astonishment, before leaving that afternoon, the subs working that day at the project, came to Larry asking what they could do to get things started.

The plumbing and air conditioning subs leading the way.

He explained, with help from the plumber, what all was needed early the next morning.

Larry arrived before daybreak the next day. No surprise to him, men from the subs had already pumped out the water, started excavating, while shoring up the walls of the very deep trench needed for the repair.

Even some local folks not affiliated came to offer help.

By noon on Thursday, working in knee-deep mud, he had cut out the split section of pipe. Ends cleaned up and ready for the repair.

Now comes the part where a welder needs to weld in a small new section of pipe.

Understand, this size pipe required an excavator or crane to lift and maneuver such heavy items down into the trench and into position for installing.

The operator who would be operating the excavator to lift and lower items into the trench was an elderly gentleman in blue jean style overalls.

When he arrived, he just back up close, then went down into the trench to talk to the workers down in the trench.

They spent a few minutes talking, but unless you were down in the trench, it was all muffled, not understandable from above. Really didn't matter.

In just a short time, he climbs the ladder out and walks out to a truck before coming back to help with the lifting.

Broken pieces lifted out in no time.

Now for the pipe, that is another issue. Pipe of that size just aren't laying around. The cost and storage require them to be ordered per plan and specifications, with weeks if not months of before shipping and receiving on a job site.

Workers who have been here since the breakage, finally stopped not having the pipe on site to install. All pretty wasted working for over 24 hours since arriving.

Larry, looking into the faces of these men and women, felt a rush of utter pride and revived faith in how they all came together to help him out. He needed to do something for them but has had little time to come up with everything that has been going on.

Looking around, to Larry's amazement, even the subs who had a part and those who did not have to participate, stayed, and when asked why, they all just commented, "Just in case we're needed."

Night fall was coming, and Larry was trying to come up with how he could do something for everyone.

When out of nowhere he heard, "Is anyone hungry?"

Larry, turning around and looking through the crowd of people, saw who he recognized as the school's kitchen crew.

The four-person kitchen crew pulled up in an electric kart, stopped and while getting out said, "Heard we had some hungry people out here playing in the mud."

Small laughter from the large crowd, seeing how exhaustion had started taking its toll on many.

"Seeing we are all just rookies in the kitchen, thought we would use you all for a test run on our food. Any takers?"

Larry could not believe it, right behind them came the maintenance crews in their vehicles. As they pulled up, they were filled with enough food to feed an army. One cart was full of ice, and when a small portion was brushed away, it revealed an assortment of cold drinks, followed by a cart that had coffee and hot chocolate.

It took no encouragement to the many there to head over and take a break.

All joined in for food, drink, and small talk.

Great to see all the smiling faces. Well, many, dirty smiling faces.

The plumbing foreman, standing in quite a large group that had gathered, was on the cell talking to someone, asking what was the latest on the new pipe. He had little response to what he was hearing. "Yes, I see" was repeated over and over.

As he put his cell back in his pocket and looked up, he had no idea that everyone there had stopped talking and was waiting to hear what he had found out.

Larry, seeing the predicament and pressure he was under, walked up to the foreman, put his arm around him, pulling him away from everyone, walking just out of hearing range.

No one was talking, just sipping on drinks, and taking bites of food.

They all knew what was hanging on that call. It meant the difference between winning or losing.

Larry in a calm voice asks, "So what's up with the pipe?"

The foreman, who has been here since the start, has a hard time starting to talk and pauses looking at Larry.

Larry takes a breath, looks at him and says, "Look, none of this is your fault. If the pipe gets here great, if not, we'll just wait until it does and go to plan B, the diary tankers. It is a win, win scenario."

They had already placed the tankers on site at a location where the building could be bypassed and water tanker, hooked up.

The foreman cleared his voice, just talked to my guy in the office at home, he says so far, he has not found any pipe that size and specifications that can be here in time to get it installed.

Larry gave him a hug, telling him, you and everyone here has gone above and beyond to help.

As Larry reaches over to console the foreman seeing he is almost to tears, he sees the excavator operator walking over. Larry holds up his hand to stop him, but he keeps coming.

Larry, being a little perturbed by this action, asks him, "What is it you want," releasing the foreman and approaching the operator.

The operator responds, "It seems to me, now that we all have had some food and drink, we should get back to finishing the job."

Larry, shaking his head disgustingly, says, "Well so happens, it's what we were just talking about, and if you must know, we have no pipe." Larry tries to control his emotions. He notices some activity in the direction of the group around the food carts.

"Well then," the operator starts talking, "I noticed a truck just pulled up and I believe he has something for you guys."

Larry and the foreman walk towards the crowd that has now gathered around the large truck.

As they get closer, they see a very large pipe in the back tied down with chains.

Larry, in astonishment, asks the driver of the truck, "What is going on?"

The driver replies, "Well couple hours ago we got a call. This guy told us that a piece of pipe will be delivered in just a short time. He needs it cut down to this certain length, then he gave us an address where to deliver it. He said you guys might be needing this."

Larry asks, "Who is this guy?"

Driver, "I'm sorry, he told us he would send over four thousand dollars to be split equally between us. Seeing it arrived and only two of us there, a thousand dollars an hour was a pretty good deal, so I asked no more questions and there you are."

Driver, "He also said thanks for letting him run the excavator."

All the while the foreman is up in the back of the truck measuring the pipe.

The foreman yells out, "Larry, it is perfect, it will work."

Larry, looking around to get a glimpse of the elderly gentlemen, saw nothing but the taillights of his truck going down the street.

The foreman now coming over to Larry asks, "Who did this?"

Larry, looking in the direction of an empty seat in the excavator, replies, "Just an old friend."

Larry goes over, gets in the excavator, and yells out, "Let's get this pipe in the trench."

They had the main line repaired and water flowing by the next day.

You can imagine the relief and self-gratification Larry felt as he walked down the hallway Monday the opening morning of school, knowing the miracle that had taken place earlier.

He could hear all the sounds a school makes listening as he passed by each open classroom door, children laughing, reading out answers to questions, asking questions, and teachers doing their part in educating our youth.

Just about halfway down the hall leading to the main office Larry heard a loud alarm going off and it seemed like all hell was about to break loose, but in fact it was the school's first fire drill.

The halls filling up as teachers lead their classes in a highly organized way out of the classrooms and down the halls, to clearly marked exiting doors, Larry just stood back against the wall and enjoyed the sounds surrounding him, smiling but also having that deep burn going on inside.

The hallways now empty and quiet, Larry gets back to business, deciding to go to the main office to be sure everything operated the way it was supposed to in a fire drill.

As he entered the office, a young woman, who seemed confused, runs into Larry.

She stepped back not looking into Larry's eyes and apologized for her blunder.

Larry chuckling, "Where is the fire?"

She looks up at Larry and laughing says, "Well technically here."

"What's the rush and aren't you going in the wrong direction, Miss?" he asks.

"Well in all the hurry, I forgot the roll call sheet in my classroom that we are supposed to have with us to verify we have all our students."

"That sounds important to me, but if you are in here, who is watching your class out there?" again smiling.

"Oh, that's not a problem, we have assistants who help us out and with all the teachers, we cover for each other."

"Well, that's comforting to know and if I ever have a kid in this school, I'll feel good knowing you and all your helpers have it under control," smiling.

She asks, "Who are you and what exactly are you doing here?"

"Well, I am the guy who has spent the last three months getting your classroom ready for you so you can be the great teacher I know you are."

She thanks him for his compliment but says, "Really you do not even know me."

"Well, I know this for sure, someone who would run back into a burning building to get the right paperwork is OK by me," laughing out loud as she joins in laughing as well.

Just then, they get all clear to return to their classes.

In a panicked voice she says, "Oh my god I must get back, so thanks and I hope to see you around" as she runs down the hall to her classroom. Just as she is ready to enter her door she stops and yells out, "Oh and by the way, I have a wall plug that does not work. Can you get someone to look at it?"

He turns back to look at her. "You bet I can. What is your room number and when the drill is over? I'll get right on it."

"Room 140! Thanks!"

Larry, now feeling better than he has felt for a long time, goes to his job trailer and pages up the electrician. He comes by and tells him of the problem with the wall outlet. He asks him to look at its ASAP; he agrees.

The last day, the day Larry has been waiting for three months now has arrived, final walk through and he is gone for a month.

With Larry, a representative for the school, a foreman for every subcontractor, the engineers, the architect, and the local inspectors.

He also brings along someone to write down everything that needs attention as well, his assistant who will take care of the punch list while Larry is gone.

Seeing how this needs to be done while school is in session, the kids in each classroom get a kick out of all the attention they seemed to get when visited by the inspection group.

Each classroom takes only a few minutes, you see the administrator of the school, and seeing the teachers have been in their classrooms preparing for school to open, had all the teachers write down a list of items they felt needed attention which helped speed up the whole process.

So, as they entered the rooms, the teacher would hand them a list and if needed they would look at any major items, but for the most part it was cosmetic defects, screws missing, covers crooked, tiles out of place, all kinds of items with some rooms having not one item, quite a feat seeing the time they had to get it done.

The last room to inspect for the day was, by chance, room 140. Larry looked up and smiled knowing he would see that wacky new teacher he had run into during the fire drill.

The door was already open as the group walked in. Larry glanced around the room looking for the teacher but seeing only children and what had to be the assistant.

Again, as Larry being the last one to enter was just inside the door but out of view of the hallway, the teacher came running in and again ran into Larry knocking herself to the floor.

She looks up as Larry reaches out to help her up smiling and saying, "Another fire drill, Miss?"

She was so embarrassed. She responds, "No I heard there was an inspection coming and I didn't want to miss it, so I have been waiting all afternoon and just had to use the restroom. I am so sorry."

Larry asks, "What's your name?"

"Sue Wilson, what is yours?"

Larry replies with a complete astounding look on his face, "I once knew a Sue who was a little crazy like you too, thanks."

"Thanks for what, I did nothing but run into you twice?"

Larry smiles and asks, "Did you do your list of anything that might be wrong in your classroom?"

"Yes, I did. Mary my assistant has it all typed out and ready for you. It doesn't have much on it and oh, thanks for sending that nice man over to fix my wall plug so fast."

"My pleasure for sure feeling that burn inside increasing ever so much."

She calls out for Mary to bring Larry the list.

Larry, now back to business and knowing he is minutes away from starting his month-long search for his Sue, has an urgency come over him to get going.

He moves past his colleagues to get the list from the teacher's assistant almost in a panic mode to hurry up, the last room and he is out of there.

The architect stops him to ask him what outlet she is talking about.

"Oh, last week while they were doing a fire drill, she told me about a wall outlet that wasn't working. I had the electrician check it out and all it was, the breaker was off."

As Larry turned to get the list, he thanked the assistant for her help reading the short list and asking, "How is she as a teacher?"

The assistant replies, "About as good as I hope you are as a father."

"A strange thing to say to someone you don't know," he replies still looking at the list.

Larry looks up and standing in front of him is his Sue!

Tears running down her face and everyone in the room not even breathing you could hear a pin drop.

The teacher asks, "You two know each other?"

Larry still did not say a word but kept looking deep into Sue's eyes.

Finally, he says, "Mary, can I have word with you in private please?"

"Of course," she says, "we can go to the teachers' lounge."

Larry instructs his man to take over the inspection, tells everyone if they have any questions that his assistant can take care of it and leaves with Sue.

They enter the lounge and embrace each other and kiss like tomorrow would never come.

Sue asks, "Why call me Mary when you know my name?"

He replies, "With all that has happened I do not want to take any chances and I felt it best until we were alone," embracing again.

Sue says in a soft loving voice, "Would you like to see your daughter Tana?"

"Would I, how long to get to her. What doe she look like, what color is her hair, her eyes—oh my god I have a daughter!" he yells out.

"You should know you built this place and one of the things the school offers to its faculty is a full service, free of cost, day school right here."

She is here on the school grounds? Unbelievable—let's go now!"

They walk down the hall to the door leading into the day school. They are greeted by a faculty member, Kathy, who takes care of the kids. "You are leaving early today, Mary? I'll get Tana for you."

She walks into a room which above the door says three-year-olds and returns with the prettiest little girl Larry has ever seen.

Not wanting to scare her, Sue says, "Tana, this is Larry."

"Hi Larry," she replies.

"How are you doing, Tana?"

"Fine, I painted with watercolors today. Do you want to see?"

"Sure do," and she takes Larry by the hand and walks back into her classroom with her dad.

She stops and asks, "Mommy, is this okay? You told me to watch for danger strangers. Is this man one of those?"

Sue about to burst says, "No, Tana, that man is your daddy."

The daycare person, Kathy, walks up to Sue asking, "Is this okay to let him go with her?"

"Oh yes that is more than okay," she replies, as tears of joy run down her face. "That's her daddy." She turns and looks at Kathy, who as you might know is in total shock saying not a word.

Sue goes to join her husband and daughter for the first time as a family.

"LIFE GOES ON"

As you can imagine, the next few days are filled full of getting to know each other, both for Sue and Larry but especially for Tana now that she has her daddy.

Both dad and daughter took to each other like they had been together since the beginning.

Sue had explained to Larry that she felt inside that he would look for her until he found her so she stayed put where she was relocated so not to complicate Larry's search anymore than it must have been.

She too had been given a small but comfortable home, car, job, and bank book. She did not use much of what was given to her like Larry searching so she pretty much had the full amount still in the account.

They spent the next few days just talking and getting comfortable being back together again.

They discussed the possibilities now owning two homes just what to do knowing they really did not need two, They decided to sell Larry's home and stay in the one Sue was given.

It would be more comforting for Tana not to have to adjust to a new home.

They both had some difficulties calling each other by their new names and when asked by Tana why daddy called mommy Sue she responded with,

"Well back when mommy and daddy went to school my nickname was Sue, so daddy calls me still today."

Tana had a confused look but that quickly turned to a smile when she said, "Mommy, Sue is a pretty name, but can I still call you just mommy," in true three-year-old fashion.

Larry decided he needed to go by his house and spend a couple days cleaning up and getting a real estate company to list the house for him.

On his way driving over, which was only about an hour or so away, Larry got to thinking about the past few years and especially the past few weeks. Lots of crazy stuff he thought smiling to himself, lots of bad stuff as well.

Then it hit him, he had forgotten to let Fyfe know about finding Sue, so he tried calling but as usual he got nothing but a recording. His message was short and sweet: "By God, I found her! Thanks for all your help!"

Knowing Fyfe would understand and could go on with his life as well.

Larry's house was quite the sight being left to tend for itself over the past few years while he focused on work and finding Sue; he felt a sadness not taking care of the house and leaving it in such disarray.

Larry ,being who he was and what he does for a living, got on the phone and made some calls to his subcontractors he had used on the Charter School, to help him renovate the home, so the next lucky family buying the house could enjoy the home from the day they got the title.

He completely stripped the floors and redid them all. Completely repainted inside and out, tore out all the cabinets and appliances and installed state-of-the-art appliances, new oak cabinets, and marble countertops.

He had the front and back yards completely reseeded and fresh new bushes and trees planted.

It was a pretty sight to see when he completed it a few weeks later.

He even brought Sue and Tana over when after only a week on the market it sold for full asking price, to look at what he had done.

Sue commented, "Nicer than the one we live in now," cracking a smile.

Larry at that instant realized he might have gone just a tad overboard.

While walking around the home, the real estate agent had arrived with information for Larry where he was to go and sign the final papers and pick up a check.

He knew not to introduce Sue and Tana as his wife and daughter, so he grabbed up Tana and whispered in her ear, "Daddy is going to play a game with this nice lady, so you play along with daddy, ok?"

Tana whispered back, "Ok, daddy, does mommy know how to play?"

"She sure does. We will be using our nicknames, but you can use your name, Tana," smiling at her.

Larry puts her down and turns to talk to the real estate broker and introduce Tana and Sue to her as a college friend he had run into while doing some of the home repairs and she wanted to see the home before it was occupied.

"Greg," she replied, "is she looking to buy?"

"Oh no she has a nice home of her own a few hours away," smiling and winking at Tana.

Now everything was cool so far, but kids will be kids and Tana laughing now just having a grand old time shouts out, "Daddy, your nickname is funny!"

Holy crap, the innocents of youth.

The real estate lady looked at her funny and started to say something but stopped just short of it and just shrugged her shoulders, turned and as she was walking away waved and said, "See you at the signing."

Larry looked over at Sue and both busted out laughing. Now that was a close one.

So now on the way home, Larry got to thinking how wonderful it would be to take his family camping. "Sue," he asked, "what do you think about taking a couple of days and go camping?"

"What a wonderful idea! You know we haven't been since that day," stopping just short of saying it, but even so, silence fell over both along with a cold chill just the thought of it stirred just horrible remembrances they both would like to forget.

Larry cleared his throat. "I think we should go rent a nice RV and head to a lake and go fishing, a busy large lake with lots of campers."

"Sounds like the best thing we could do right now so let us stop by before getting home and rent one today before we have time to think on it anymore."

Little Tana asks, "What is camping, daddy?"

"Oh my, it is lots of fun. We eat lots of food, go out in a boat and catch fish, sit by a warm campfire at night and eat s'mores."

"What's s'mores, daddy?"

"It is graham crackers with chocolate and marshmallows."

"That sounds good," Tana replies.

"Ok so let's do it, deal?" looking at his girls.

They in turn look at each other and at the same time turn to Larry and say, "Deal!"

The next day while Sue prepares and stocks up the RV they rented, Larry goes into town to sign the papers and get his check. You see the buyers had already signed and the bank had issued the final check to close out the deal all on the same day.

So as the sun rises, their excitement running high, they set off for, wait just a second, Larry thinking to himself, where are we going?

He looked over at Sue and asked, "Honey, did we ever talk about where we were going camping?"

Sue, looking slightly puzzled replies, "I guess not, oh well just drive and when you figure it out just head that way," as she gets up adding, "I am going to fix us some breakfast burritos while you figure that out."

He really didn't have any idea being so far from where they grew up, but Arizona is known for all kinds of outdoor activities, so he looked out and said quietly, "That mountain range looks like it holds some promise," and off in that direction he drove.

One of the best spots for camping and fishing is up on the Tonto National Forest.

Your choices of streams and lakes are abundant.

Passing through a small town, you know, like most in the mountains, a few cafés, some small shops, and only a couple of gas stations.

Feeling just a little road-tired driving, he decided to stop at what looked like a family run burger joint, you see them in all small towns, pitched flat roofs, with wooden picnic tables out front with umbrellas, walk-up sliding windows to order, all painted white with red or blue trim, the smell of burgers and fries cooking, you just cannot resist with all senses firing at warp speed.

He orders up three picnic burger basket specials and thick chocolate shakes with whip cream and a cherry on top. Wait, as she brings the order up, he asks, "Can we get triple cherries on each, please."

She smiles and adds cherries to each shake. Then she asks, "Is there something special about the number three?"

Larry smiled and replies smiling, "It represents myself, my wife, daughter."
She replies, "Well that is great."

He grabs up the bags, gives her a wink and a big thank you, then on to the lake.

The way they devoured the burgers, fries, and shakes, you would have thought they hadn't eaten in days, but like all camping adventures, the food just tastes that much better. I was once told that it is the high altitude that does that, but really who cares.

He had seen a sign back a few miles with a couple lakes listed so he just headed in that direction.

Larry all along had this feeling that kept trying to ruin his trip, the feeling that you have missed or forgot something, the feeling you want to shake off but just quite can't.

Funny thing though, when you feel the most comfortable in life is when life usually kicks you around a bit. Hands you the Ace of Spades when you least expect it. Some people can never let their guard down knowing this fact. Example, how many times have you had just little extra money in your pocket and are feeling rather good about yourself only to have your car break down, or the washing machine start spraying water all over the house, a dentist visit turn into a full-blown root canal and cap, or a good friend in need ask for some help. You just never seem to get one step up that something comes along and knocks the wind right out of your sails. That's life.

Well as good as Larry is feeling right now, nothing could keep him from smiling.

He decides to pull into the filling station and top off before the last couple of hours driving before getting to the lake.

He stops, gets out of the RV, and starts the pump. Sticking his head inside the door, he tells Sue he wants to get a better road map of the area and will be right back.

He walks into the small convenience store at the station and looks around a bit when a lady behind the counter asks, "Can I help you with something?"

"Sure thing, I am looking for a map that shows the lakes up around this area."

"Sure thing," she says, "we have a good one, a map showing all the roads and all the lakes in the entire forest, only six bucks too, pretty good deal."

"Great," he says as he opens it up and spreads it out across the countertop. "Any one lake better than the other?"

"They are all good this time of year. You see the Game and Fish boys stock them up. This one here was stocked just over a week ago and they should be striking at bare hooks by now."

He was folding up the map and looking around at all that stuff, you know the last minute got to have junk they have at the counter, that impulse stuff you just must grab something, even though you don't really need.

The front door opens and in walks the guy delivering the daily paper, so he grabs one and says, "Add this as well."

He pays for his items, goes back, hangs up the hose, tosses the stuff over on the passenger seat, fires up the RV and heads to the lake.

An hour or so goes by when Sue comes forward and grabs the stuff off the seat and says, "Little miss was so tired she is back there sound asleep."

Sue reaches down for the map, glances over it and tosses it up on the dash, picks up the paper and starts to read some of the local gossip.

"We should be at the lake in about an hour," Larry says, and kind of singing, "cannot wait to get a fire going, get out the chocolate, the grahams, and the marshmallows."

He glances over at Sue and notices tears running down her face. "Honey, what is wrong?"

She slowly turns to look at Larry not saying a word.

"Sue, what's wrong?" he asks again.

She shows Larry the headlines of the paper: 'FBI Agents Killed While Transporting Convicted Mob Hit Man.'

Larry pulls off the side of the road. Sue still has not said a word. He slowly takes the paper from her grasping hands and reads, "Agent Bernard Fyfe was one of three FBI agents killed while transporting convicted mob hit man Frank Mast to a hearing where Mast was to give witness about other mob related crimes. It is now believed that Mast had completely been setting this up for some three years waiting on his appeal hearing giving testimony only to Agent Fyfe. In all, three FBI agents were killed and one seriously injured.

"The injured agent told first responders, 'We had stopped at the train crossing waiting for the train to pass in the early morning hours, when four men appeared from an abandoned rail car off at a side switch.' They came running at them using large caliber weapons to first blast out the windows and then turned them on the agents at close range. 'It happened so fast; I did not even get my weapon unholstered.' He passed out and is still in critical condition in an induced coma."

Larry sits back. "I cannot believe he's gone, such a great guy, just doing what he loved." He looks at Sue who now looks to be in total shock.

She says in a low voice asking, "It will never end will it, will it?"

He did not know what to say glancing toward the back of the RV making sure Tana was still napping.

"Can Frank really be that horrible of a person to have planned it all out? Unbelievable, just unbelievable."

Now his thought patterns go in the direction remembering what Frank had told him how he would get to him and his family. There is no place to hide.

Can he really find them after all these years and being in a different part of the country?

His first concerns: Sue, and Tana, get them where it is safe.

He thinks a bit and tells her to relax and that they will spend the night at the lake and come up with a game plan.

Not saying a word, she nods approval.

Arriving at the lake, they don't start a campfire, don't get out the goodies but lock themselves in for the night.

The evening air crisp, the smell of pine trees, and burning campfires lingering should have had Larry feeling very relaxed, not having a care in the world except to take care of his family, but now the horrible news has him getting all knotted up inside, just like during the trial and trying to find Sue.

In the morning and not being able to sleep, he gets up and makes some coffee.

Sue and Tana managed to sleep so he tried not to wake them, letting them sleep until they are done.

He sips his coffee with thoughts of what to do filling his head.

He grabs up the paper and reads through it again trying to pick out any points that might be of some help, nothing.

Now understand this, they are totally alone in this fight for life, the only one who might could help is gone.

FBI, local police, CIA, not a soul would believe their story and who can they trust? They stand alone against a man who as it seems has everything going for him.

Sure, he has all law enforcement agencies again looking for him, but Frank won't make any mistakes this time, he has had years to plan this one out.

Will he spend the time to get me as he had stated; does he have the resources to do such a search with so many looking for him at the same time?

Larry nods his heads. I am sure he does and will; he has nothing to lose.

With that thought planted in his head, Sue and Tana walk out, Tana smiling as she sees her daddy and Sue looking like she had not slept at all.

He gets up and makes a cup of coffee for her and a bowl of cereal for Tana.

Sitting quietly sipping their coffee, Sue looks up and asks, "So what do you think we should do?"

"Well, I thought all night long. First, spend a few days here at the lake, then go home and do what normal families do and that is continue our new lives."

She looks confused then an expression of relief to now understand what he was saying but not saying.

"Live our lives like normal people. If Frank is going to get his revenge, we will not even know it. That is his way like he said; his victims do not even know it was him who ended their lives."

Larry tried to recall anything that might help him protect his family; then like a cool breeze in summer, he recalled what Frank had implied. He is not after the family, but only me, recalling when Sue had her day to testify, Frank's attorney declined and asked her no questions, yet another move on Frank's part to single out the person who put him in prison, Larry.

At least now he knew Frank would not harm Sue or Tana but could use them to get to him.

As the days rolled by, it got easier and easier to do just that, live out their lives.

Life has a way to even brighten up the worst situations.

Larry has been making multiple precautions installing state of the art alarm system in the house, cameras covering all areas outside, and get a handgun but put it out of harm's way so not to endanger Tana.

Deep down he always has that feeling knowing somewhere out their Frank was observing, planning, and his next moves.

One day Larry got this idea that maybe they should move to a completely different part of the country, maybe even another country, so he sat down and planned things out before he approached Sue.

He knew if they were going to relocate, he wanted to do it before Tana went to school which was not that long into the future.

So, after weeks of figuring all angles, he went to Sue and laid his plan out.

Up to now he still was not sure if it was the right thing to do, but then he realized that the past few weeks while he strategized, he stopped thinking about Frank and focused on his family, and plan to relocate. At this moment he knew without a doubt it was the best thing to do.

He was not sure how she was going to take it seeing she has time at this home, and Tana going to school.

Sue put Tana to bed as usual and Larry waited out on the porch for her sipping on some wine he had picked up earlier that day.

He knew how much she enjoyed a glass, so he had one already poured for her along with some nice cheese to munch on.

The screen door opened, and she walked out, paused at what she saw and gave him a big bear hug and a loving kiss.

"What's up?" she asked.

"Well, I have been doing some thinking and have spent some time doing some planning and was wondering what would you think about moving?"

She sipped on some wine, looked up at him and said, "I love you dearly and will go wherever you feel we should go, but if the reason is only to avoid what we know will happen eventually then I am not sure if it is the right thing to do."

"I am not sure what you mean by that," he replied.

"Well, if he still is after us as we both agree he is, then does it really matter where we live?"

He sat for a minute thinking of what she said and how true it was what she said.

He takes a breath and says, "It is part of the reason but just let me tell you this, while I was thinking of the move and all that it involves along with the excitement of a new place, I totally forgot about Frank," smiling at her.

Sue sipped some more wine while glancing across the front yard, stopping to swirl her wine around inside the glass, looking up at Larry and saying,

"It sounds like a good idea, with what we have in savings from the sale of your house and with both of us working, we have a sizable amount, enough to go a long ways, not to forget selling this house and what we would get out of it. We would have enough to buy a new home and live comfortable while we look for employment. Now for the million dollar question, where are you thinking?"

"I have always wanted to live by water, either a lake, stream, or ocean, preferably in the mountains, a small town that with my construction skills would fit it and a school system for you to apply at."

"Sounds like you got it well planned, but where do you think?"

"Well for all around location I was thinking right here in Northern Arizona; it is a growing area and has plenty of medical facilities, shopping, schools, along with all kinds of outdoor activities which we all love to do. I checked it out and some areas have some fine gated communities to give us a bit more security as well. Let us take a run up there within the month and see. Better yet, let's rent an RV and spend a couple of weeks driving the northern part of the state and see. Maybe some other nice spot might hit us both."

They both agreed to put in for the time off and with that went to bed and slept about as well as they have in years.

In the weeks leading up to setting out, Larry decided to buy an RV instead of renting. He did not tell Sue, just showed up with it one afternoon after work.

It was nice with an on the self-adjusting satellite system, plenty of room for three, and two slide outs for additional room.

She asks, "Why buy?"

"Well as crazy as it sounds, we may have to live in this thing while we look around for a new home when we pick a spot to relocate, and we'll have something to take us to all the great camping spots we want without the hassle of getting room reservations and having to stop for meals along the way."

"Well, it's not like we can't afford it. Great decision, and gives him a big hug and kiss."

He was excited about his new RV and spent quite a lot of time getting everything one hundred percent ready; he did not want Tana or Sue to have any reasons not to want to move or travel around.

The day was coming soon when they would be leaving for a couple of weeks and Larry needed just a few more items at the local RV Center.

A strange thing happened when he was leaving the parking lot. A van seemed to follow him all the way home but turning just before reaching his home.

He thought, man am I paranoid or what. Am I going to watch everything now as if they are following me? Don't think so.

But in the days to follow, he saw that van in numerous locations either parked or seemed like it followed him only to turn off before reaching his house.

One time he pulled into the driveway, turned around and went back to the street it turned down, but the van wasn't to be seen.

All along he said nothing to Sue; her excitement level was up so high he took in on himself and decided like he had done in the past to handle it himself.

The day came for their trip to start so he gathered up his family and headed north.

Everything was going fine for the first half hour or so, but again, right before he was to enter the freeway north, he glanced in his mirror to be sure things were clear, and back about a hundred yards or so was that van.

He watched as he sped up to get on the freeway. The van headed up the access road as if to come up alongside of them.

Larry's heart was pounding as the van drew closer and closer in anticipation; he thought he might get a glimpse of the driver, but just as it got within a few feet, the van turned off the freeway.

Larry was sweating so hard Sue asked him if he was alright. He nodded yes with a subdued smile.

Well, their week or so of traveling around was great, checking out houses and all the fun and exciting outdoor activities offered in the different locations.

All in all, they drove over 1,000 miles in a two-week period covering a large area.

Sue needed to get back to work as well as Larry. Tana was starting school herself this year as well.

With that in mind, Larry was growing anxious to decide and make the move prior to her starting school. He knew once she started, every day after would make it harder and harder for Sue to go along for the relocation.

When he returned to work, he requested any projects that might be in the areas he was looking to relocate so he would have time to further his investigation.

His boss, Scott, asked, "Why do you want to be away from your young family?"

Larry had to think hard on this one; he didn't want Scott to know he wanted to relocate so he came up with this thought that he shared with him: "Well I have been with you guys for some time now and feel like family here so I was thinking of an idea to help you expand your business. So while I would be doing these project, I could spend some time looking for more opportunities as well for you guys."

Scott was totally grateful and even excited about what Larry had suggested. He told Larry that if he found something that would work, he would be a partner in that location, fifty percent partner!

Scott even went on to tell Larry to take the next few weeks and go check things out and they would even reimburse him for his cost as well as full compensation while gone.

On the way home, Larry got to thinking more about what he had said to him. He realized even though at the time it was a way for him to keep from telling Scott the real reason that it might be a real solution.

For one thing he would once again be the man in charge and build something for his family's future.

When he arrived at home that day, he could not wait to tell Sue the great news.

She could not believe it herself but helped Larry the next day pack up so he could head out to spend more time looking for a new business location and a new home for his family. Things seem to be looking bright.

In the past few days, Larry had not seen the van and again thought maybe he was just being over cautious.

He did have moments of indecision about leaving his family alone for any amount of time, but remembering what Frank had told him long ago, he knew hurting his family was not Frank's style, so off he went.

He spent a few days around central areas of Arizona and then decided to head farther north checking out numerous small and some sizable towns along the way.

Each town had good points and bad; all of them would be great to raise a family but lacked enough work to start a business, so onward weary traveler.

It was in a small restaurant eating breakfast outside of Flagstaff, man this place was crazy on portions of food, half pound of bacon, hash browns, three eggs, juice, and coffee for ten bucks. Well anyway, while enjoying his meal, it occurred to him that he might be going about this wrong. He was looking at one town big enough for the business but what about a town that was centrally located between a bunch of smaller towns? It makes all the sense in the world, so he asked the waitress if they had a map and sure enough they did just for travelers, a single sheet map but it was perfect listing only sites of interest and different towns between.

He studied for some time and then it hit him—Cottonwood. It is within a short drive of Phoenix as well as Flagstaff, Sedona, Camp Verde, to name a few, millions of people, and potential customers. It was perfect.

He headed there to check it out and what he found was just what the doctor ordered.

A small-town atmosphere, centrally located, nice schools, shopping, and a mega of outdoor pleasures within reach.

His mind was spinning with ideas and the hopes that Jim would agree to back him in this new venture.

Time as you know was running out, so this thing had to happen or it wasn't going to happen at all; Tana starts school in a month.

When he arrived back home, he told Sue all about Cottonwood and they spent the night looking at everything they could find on Cottonwood from the history to schools, shopping, recreation, weather, left no stone unturned you might say. They agreed this could be the place for them.

Now the kicker is if Larry can get Scott to go along with the idea and just how quickly he would let Larry move on it.

The rest of the night went by slowly for him in anticipation of how to swing this deal with Scott.

He went over everything he could looking at the good stuff and what to counter with on any bad stuff.

He wanted to be thorough and complete with his presentation so instead of trying to sleep, he got up and started writing down all his ideas and thoughts and categorized them in a formal presentation.

Before you knew it, he heard his alarm go off and rushed to shut it down before it woke everyone up.

He had not taken but a couple of weeks, so he didn't want Scott to think he hadn't thought this thing out all the way. His game plan was to get into the office at the normal time, make his presence known to everyone and in passing by, tell Scott he'll have some ideas to go over after he looks into a few other items.

He did just that, gathered more information and did some financial planning. Remember Larry had his own company before so this was not new to him.

Later that day after lunch, Scott walked by Larry's office and asked, "When do you want to sit down and go over your plan?"

He responded, "Well if it works for you, what I really would like to do is maybe finish out the day working on it and then you and I could meet at the steak house, get a bite, and spend some time going over it."

"That sounds like a good idea, so let us say we will meet at six."

"Six works great for me. I will have some time to go by the house first to let Sue know what's going on. See you then."

Larry, finishing off the day a bit early, races home to tell Sue his plans and she eagerly agrees.

He stops in on Tana to give his girl a big hug and kiss and spend a few minutes before leaving.

He is feeling the best he has felt since finding his girls some time ago.

He leaves heading towards the entrance to the freeway when he spots the van sitting off the side of the road.

Slowing down as he passes, he tries to get a look inside, but the windows are so darkly tinted he sees nothing but his own vehicle's reflection in the side window.

He speeds up hoping he was not spotted and stops at the entrance lights at the freeway, you know the ones that only allow one vehicle at a time.

The wait seems like minutes but is only a few seconds.

Green light for him and so he accelerates off from the light. After just a few feet he glances into his rear-view mirror and sees the van pulling in line a few cars back.

Racing through what was some really backed-up traffic, he felt he had put plenty of distance between himself and the van to focus more on the task ahead of him with Scott.

He arrives at the restaurant to find Scott already waiting for him inside at a table.

Not realizing he had worked up a sweat, Scott asked, "What the heck, did you jog over here or drive?"

Larry had a deer in the headlights look and asked, "What do you mean?"

"Well, you have sweat running down your forehead, my friend," chuckling while sipping on a glass of wine.

"Oh, I just had a real close call on the freeway, and I am still upset a bit I guess," he explained.

Scott tells Larry, "I have been here before so I took it upon myself to order us up an incredibly special steak dinner with all the trimmings so we can eat and get down to business, alright with you?"

"You bet it is. Waiter, can I get an ice water and a cold draft beer please?"

As he walks by, "Sure thing, sir, coming right up," he replies with a smile.

Scott and Larry have a wonderful meal and discuss all kinds of topics while finishing up.

Scott says, "Well now that the feast bag is off, let's have it, buddy."

Larry starts in and does not stop for over an hour, all the while watching Scott's expressions and body movements to get some kind of idea what he may be thinking.

"Well, that's it in a nutshell," says Larry.

Scott picks up his glass of wine, takes a sip, another sip, sets his glass down and says, "A nutshell, a pretty big nutshell I would say. I wish all of my partners were as thorough as you are, heck I wouldn't have to do a damn thing. When can you relocate and get this thing off the ground and flying?"

"Within the month for sure. You want to go over anything, funding, structure, anything?"

"No, sir, I do not. I will get with accounting first thing in the morning to get the required accounts set up within the week."

Scott stands up proudly, reaches out his hand to Larry, and while giving him a firm handshake says, "I am proud to be partners with you and feel with you running this new part of our company that we will be very successful in the years to come."

They walk out into now an almost empty parking lot seeing it is now very late into the night.

Again, Scott shakes Larry's hand. As he sits into his car, Larry shuts the door and waits while Scott backs out waiving to him as he leaves.

Larry is so excited; he cannot wait to tell Sue the news and start planning their move to Cottonwood.

Larry walks over to his car, reaches to open the door and in glancing sees the van parked over in a parking lot adjacent to the restaurant's parking lot.

He quickly gets in, starts up the car and speeds away all the while watching for the van in his mirrors.

The next morning, he gets up earlier than usual and makes Sue and Tana a Sunday breakfast on Thursday.

He would occasionally look outside to see if the van is around, nothing.

The girls get up and to their surprise sit down for a great early morning breakfast of blueberry pancakes, eggs, bacon, and orange juice.

He tells them all about his meeting and that they will be moving within the next few weeks.

A brand-new start for his family, exciting for everyone.

The days sped by while preparing to move, furniture all gone and, on its way, to their new home that was not ready for them. They found a home that had been used as an office for a newly developed gated community. All lots had been sold so in the deal, Larry has them doing a once over to give it that new home smell.

Later that day, they would be following up spending a night at a Cottonwood RV park for some time. You see the furniture would not arrive until the following day, but with the renovation not quite done, they would have to use the RV for a few days.

Checking to be sure everything was in order and securing the for sale sign out in the front lawn, they headed down the road.

It was not but an hour or so when he saw the van following a few hundred yards back.

He watched for quite some time being sure it was the van all along knowing he had to come up with some plan to evade whoever it was. He didn't want whoever to follow them Cottonwood.

Larry came up with an idea, so he stopped at a local filling station convenience store like the thousands all around the country.

Watching the van all the time to be sure they followed him, stopping some distance away but very visible from the store.

Sue asks, "What are we stopping here for?"

"Oh, I just wanted to get a soda for the road. You guys want anything?"

Both shaking their heads no, he walked into the store heading back to the restrooms.

He calls 911 and reports that there is a suspicious van with four men appearing to be casing the store as if to be planning to rob it. He knew that if he had said a single person only a single officer would show up, so four men seemed more threatening.

The operator thanked him for this information and told him officers were on their way.

He no sooner paid for his soda and walked out of the front door when four squad cars encircled the van.

He didn't know, but this location had a history of robberies with almost no success capturing the bad guys, so all the officers in this area were on high alert.

Larry wanted to stick around to see who was in the van but instead loaded up and sped away. The girls never knew about any of this going on.

So off to their new home and a new start in life and now hopefully, no van following them around.

A few months go by, and they all settle in with Tana loving her new school and newly found friends. Sue lands a new job just a few blocks from Tana's school at a day care center.

Larry had his office up and running and landing a few projects to kick things off. Life is good.

Larry also hadn't seen the van since the store that day when they were driving here; he felt he had finally rid himself of that lurking demon for good, but deep inside he knew if it was Frank that he would never stop until he completed what he set out to do. This kept Larry on edge and very cautious in all his and the family's activities.

Tana was driven to school even though most of her friends took a bus.

When he had the time and was around, he went with Sue to the stores, she thought he was being kind, not knowing about the van.

One day while at work, Larry had finished up early and recalled it being a day off for Sue and no school for Tana so he called her up to see if the two of them would like to do something special.

He first called her cell number, no answer, then called the house, no answer.

Larry started to get a bad feeling something was wrong.

He ran by his receptionist telling her he would be out the rest of the day and to take messages.

All the way home, his head went to spinning thinking of all the things Frank had said over the past years.

Arriving at home, he pulls into the driveway; he hit the garage door button.

To his surprise Sue's car is in the garage. His anxiety level hits the roof!

He slams on his brakes and before his truck stops, he throws it in gear and jumps out leaving the door open.

As he reaches for the door handle, he pauses. What should I do if Frank is in the house and has my girls?

He slowly turns the handle and opens the door listening for any sounds from inside.

He hears nothing but the sound of the TV.

He slowly walks through the laundry room and kitchen all the time listening for any unusual or at this point sounds at all.

The house except for the TV is uncommonly quiet.

He makes his way through the family room glancing at the TV noticing a freshly made lunch for two sitting on the small table in front of the TV.

Heart rate increasing and starting to sweat, he continues down the hall to the bedrooms glancing in them as he walks by.

When he gets to the master bedroom, he hears Tana talking in a whisper but cannot make out what she is saying, then Sue's voice at the same whisper level.

He makes his way through the master bedroom picking up a bat behind the door he keeps for unwanted intruders.

He walks slowly towards the bathroom door raising the bat like a 300-slugger in the World Series.

Just as he gets to the door, both Sue and Tana scream!

Larry swings into action getting ready to nail anything that gets in his way.

He jumps into the doorway yelling as loud as he can hoping to cause some confusion and somewhat surprising whoever is in there with his girls.

He's screaming, the girls are screaming but no one else in the bathroom.

Holding the bat over his head he yells out, "What are you screaming about?"

They reply, "What are you screaming about?"

"I called and got no answer from your cell or house phone and thought maybe something happened to you two lowering the bat."

"Are you two alone?"

"Well, I hope so, we just got back from the pharmacy."

"So, what was all the screaming about?"

"Well Tana and I just found out she was going to have a baby brother or sister, you nut."

"Oh, okay, I—what did you just say?"

"You're going to be a daddy again," smiling and Tana running and grabbing her daddy's leg.

Larry felt a rush of complete love fall over himself.

He grabbed Sue and picked up Tana and gave them both hugs and would not let go.

Sue, not quite sure what had just happened, just let it slide and they celebrated by going on a picnic, something they had not done for some time.

Tana was sure she grabbed up her favorite drinks and snacks while Larry and Sue prepared a great picnic basket.

Larry said, "Heck, we will just take an extra 30-minuete drive and go to the river so I'm grabbing a fishing rod and tackle."

Sue smiled seeing how he now seemed at ease and excited about spending the rest of the day together.

Later that month, Sue set an appointment to go get checked out to reassure that everything was going along as could be.

They did all the testing, ultrasound to be sure all was going well.

The doctor walks in saying, "You are in the best of health. What made you go and buy a pregnancy test?"

Sue replies, "Well I missed my monthly cycle and just thought it might be the stress from relocating," as Sue tells the doctor some of the past few weeks' experiences.

"Well, that would be somewhat stressful for sure," he replies. "You are quite on your way into this pregnancy already, almost three months."

"My," Sue says, "that is quite some time. Anything else?"

Just as the doctor was about to tell her, she says, "Stop, I don't want to know the sex. We didn't know on the first one, so let's just keep that going on the second."

The doctor says smiling, "I was not going to tell you the sex of the baby."

Sue looking somewhat puzzled asks, "Is everything okay?"

The doctor replies, "Everything is doubly okay!"

Sue, with her head down and in deep thought, raises her head, has that deer in the headlights look, takes a deep breath, and asks, "What do you mean doubly okay?"

"Well you are having twins, my dear," the doctor replies smiling.

Sue started to cry, not tears of anguish but tears of total love and joy.

The doctor asks, "So you don't want to know the sex?"

"Nope," she replies, "my husband will have enough to handle just knowing we are having twins."

Sue wants to pick a good time to let Larry know about the twins, so she decides to wait to tell him and Tana.

She arrives home glowing, that glow that all women have when carrying a child but, in this case, double up.

Arriving back at home, she sees Larry outside walking towards the car and asking, "Well, how did it go?"

Sue is just bursting to tell him, but she holds back. "Everything is okay, well on course," she says.

Larry looks at her saying, "You sure look like a kid who just robbed the cookie jar."

Sue, "Oh, only glad to be home and knowing we all are getting on with our lives."

As the time goes by, it gets easier to forget about the horrible past, focusing on family and business.

Larry's new business is going well. Sue can stay at home now and tend to the family. Tana is now starting third grade and her little brother is terrorizing the house.

Larry was at work one day, kind of a slow day after closing out one of many projects they had going on, reviewing contracts of future projects.

He had a case of déjà vu, something familiar happens but not quite sure what and why.

Feeling like he had already done this but not sure when or where.

He kept reviewing contracts but went back to one, a new shopping mall.

Quite a large project, but there seemed to be some hidden connection until it hit him, years ago how all their troubles seemed to start with a contract for a new shopping mall.

Unlike the past one, this was straight forward, no crazy after-hours meetings, no envelopes under the door, no pre-hired accountants to tend to business.

Recalling back then, just surviving was a full-time job, so when the opportunity for him to grab that major project came about, he thought all was good, but it really turned out all bad.

The more he thought on those past circumstances, the more none of it made sense.

Never since then have any of his businesses been offered a free accountant, weird hours, for signing a contract.

What is the common denominator that keeps puzzling him about this new comparing the old?

Of course, he never did get the chance to even get the project out of the ground; it made him wonder if the project ever happened at all.

So, he started researching the project name and did find out it did get started and completed years after.

He then wondered whatever happened to Chuck, Ben, and Bill, the money behind the project?

Why keep looking into something you've spent so much time and heartache trying to forget? Curiosity mainly to try and see why this had him interested in finding out.

Frank must have moved on, no news or sightings of him in years.

Here is the deal, it would be a closure of sorts to know what happened to the guys that were at the start of all the craziness.

Larry starts the search, first the shopping mall to see who the owners were and their connection with the three he knew of but not necessarily the owners.

Two of the three were listed as officers of the corporation, Chuck and Bill, but not Ben.

He did then run individual research on Ben alone. Days and weeks went by with no results.

Then one day he thought, maybe Ben was short for Benjamin. He got a hit, not one he thought it would be.

Benjamin J. Kenney, a known money laundering ring operator. Married with no children, also goes by the nickname, Ben.

He also read, he was found shot to death along with a close friend; no clues or evidence were found at the site for a reason why or possible motive for this killing.

Police suspected Benjamin's criminal past records showed connection with Chicago's mafia families racketeering businesses.

A well-known hit man for the families, Frank Mast, was arrested, put on trial, convicted, and found guilty on two charges of first-degree murder. He was sentenced to death but was assisting the FBI on possible convictions of other mainland mafia leaders in the hopes of getting his sentencing reduced to a life in prison in helping the FBI.

Frank Mast escaped while being transported to another facility. Four federal officers were killed and one injured. Frank Mast is still on the loose and is considered number one on the FBI's Most Wanted List.

As they say, small world. Larry now realizes the web he got himself into dealing with Ben on the shopping mall and then by accidently witnessing his murder by Frank. Not sure if Frank even realized the connections or anyone else.

Now Larry can close that chapter in his life, not sure if he should tell Sue, so as in the past, he keeps this info to himself for now.

Some time goes by, and Sue has yet to tell Larry and Tana about the twins.

As you may realize, she is now quite large and every day Larry gets more suspicious on her adding so much weight. He comments quite a lot, "I know you are eating for two, but is this weight gain normal?"

Remember Larry was not around when she was having Tana.

Sue uses this to her advantage; she comments, "This is normal. I put on more weight than normally seeing I am big boned. I weighed about the same with Tana."

Larry just shrugs his shoulders and moves on.

During the last few days before the coming of the twins, Sue starts to feel sharp pains but just works through them and tells Larry, "This is normal, not to worry."

One day, after Larry gets off early, he calls Sue and tells her, "I will stop and pick up Tana from school and will be home right after."

Tana loves ice cream, so he stops by a gas station that has softy style ice cream, dipped in chocolate with nuts sprinkled on top.

Arriving home, Larry and Tana enter the house through the garage.

Walking through the laundry room then past a large pantry and into the kitchen, he gets a whiff of a familiar odor coming from the stove top. He cannot resist, so he lifts the lid and sure enough it is Sue's chicken and dumplings.

Even Tana notices and comments how the house smells so good when mommy cooks.

Still not seeing Sue yet, Tana runs to her room yelling, "Mommy, I am home."

Still in the kitchen, Larry gets a chill when Sue does not respond, so Larry yells out, "Sue, we are home and ready for your chicken and dumplings," smiling a forced smile.

No answer from Sue. Larry goes into a full search and find mode, running by Tana's room, stops, sees she is going through some toys, heads towards the master bedroom slowing to try and hear any sounds before entering.

He slowly pushed back the door, trying not to make a sound. As the door swings open, he glances around the room. Nothing seems to be out of place. He with a low voice says, "Sue, are you here?" No answer. He walks by the large closet, which is partially open. Sue is not there. He enters the large bathroom; she is not there.

As he races back down the hallway, he stops and ponders, something was not right in the bedroom, not sure what.

He turns to go back down the hall. The door is still open. He steps in and looks over the bedroom trying to sense what's wrong.

Then like a bolt of lightning, it hits him—the overnight bag. They had set up a bag ahead of time with things she would need when having the baby.

He grabs Tana. Not knowing what is going on, she asks, "What's wrong, daddy?"

"Little missy, I think your mommy is having our baby right now and daddy is not going to miss this one."

She yells with excitement as they jump into the truck and head to the hospital that they had arranged to have the baby.

All Larry could think about is how he missed out on Tana's birth, and he was praying to God, please don't let this happen again.

They arrive in minutes, rushing into the emergency entrance, up to the receptionist. She says with a smile, I" will bet you two are looking for someone named Sue?"

Larry took a deep breath. "Yes, is she okay?"

"Where is my mommy?" Tana asks.

"Hold on, she is doing fine. Go up the maternity ward and floor number three and they'll get you right to her."

The elevator ride seemed to take hours but was less than a minute; the doors opened to the sound of babies crying.

Larry's first thought, I missed it again, lowering his head, as if in shame for once again failing to be there for his baby's birth.

As he looks around, he notices other family standing by an open door, celebrating the births of their new loved ones.

Larry and Tana walked down the hall slowly, looking at the name tags on the doors looking for Sue.

A door with no name but left slightly open, he heard Sue's voice.

He pushed back the door, and there she was, laying back. You could see the joy in her eyes as she saw Tana and Larry come through the door.

They approached and Tana casually asks, "Mommy, have you had my new baby brother or sister yet?"

Sue looks at Tana. "No, sweetheart, not yet, we were waiting on you." Then looking at Larry, "Waited for you to get here so you can be a part of it."

Larry, now smiling with tears of joy running down his face, came to Sue, leaned over, and kissed her so lightly on the forehead.

Sue says, "We didn't want you to miss this one," as she smiles.

Sue's doctor, having delivered hundreds of babies, calmly walks in and says, "So this is what we've been waiting for?"

Sue, "Yes, sir, the rest of the family."

Doctor, "Well it is a good-looking family, so what do you say we get on to adding more to this family?"

Sue says, "Hell yes, I have been carrying this weight around for long enough. Let's get this party started."

The doctor looks at Larry and says, "Sue says you want to be here during the births."

Larry responds, "Wild horses couldn't drag me away."

The doctor says, "Didn't think so, but the little one will have to just wait outside until we are done. This nice nurse will take care of her until we're through. Nurse, can you take Tana down the hall for a treat and wait with her?"

The nurse responds, "My pleasure, Doctor."

So off Tana goes as they start prepping for the baby to be born.

Like all doctors and nurses in the room, Larry was now in gown, cap, and mask. He wipes the sweat from Sue's forehead, rubbing her arm and shoulder, all the while talking to her letting her know he was there now and until the end of time.

The contractions now coming closer and closer together, Sue is not making a noise, but Larry can see the pain she is going through.

The doctor all along is being sure everyone in the room knows what is going on and what to do.

First Larry hears him say, "Okay, Sue, one big push please." Then, the head is exposed. "Again, Sue, one more big push."

It was like the baby wanted out and the next thing the doctor is holding up a baby.

Larry yells, "A boy or girl?"

Doctor, "A fully developed girl from what I see," handing the baby to one of the nurses.

Larry is not only full of excitement but mentally worn out, then, something wrong, the doctor is still looking and acting like he did before the baby was born.

Larry ponders what could be happening. Is this routine? Sue is laying with her eyes shut.

He bends over and whispers to Sue, "Are you okay?"

She opens her eyes with tears running off the corners. "Surprise!"

The doctor just then holds up another baby. At first Larry thought, he gave the baby to the nurse, looking over seeing her bathing a baby, then back to the doctor who by now is laughing out loud. He says, "Sue, I didn't think we could pull this off, but God willing, we did. I think Larry is in shock."

Larry was in shock, so much, he didn't say a word, just fell to his knees, as if he was outside looking up at the sky and says, "Thank you."

He stands, thanks everyone in the room, goes around giving them all warm embraces, then Sue calmly says, "Don't forget me, I'm the one who did all the hard work here you know."

Everyone laughs as Larry walks over to his wife now holding a baby under each arm.

Sue says, "Well, daddy, say hi to your girls."

Larry smiling like a proud dad starts to reach down but stops, looks at Sue and says, "I have one little thing yet to do. Be right back."

Larrry leaves, running down the hall to the waiting room; he looks through the glass window and sees Tana, watching TV sitting next to the nurse.

He walks through the door. She looks up and says, "Daddy, do we have a baby brother or sister?"

Larry replies, "Well why don't we go to mommy's room and check it out."

Tana runs over and jumps into Larry's arms. He hugs her and says, "Mommy has a big surprise for you."

As he turns to thank the nurse for watching Tana, in sure utter fear, death itself, there stands Frank, in a nurse's uniform even with an official name tag from the hospital.

Tana says, "Daddy, why are you squeezing me so hard? Let's go see mommy."

Larry is frozen stiff with fear. What would Frank do?

Frank walks over to Larry who still has Tana in a bear hug with her back to Frank.

Frank looks Larry directly in the eyes, those cold dark lifeless eyes. He says, "Now is not the time. Enjoy what you have left in your short life to get things right, then I will see you one last time." He opens the door and walks away.

Larry stands there, Tana saying, "Daddy, let's go see mommy."

Everything Larry had worked for, and thought would happen, is now turning the full circle.

Frank is giving time, as he said, to get things right.

Larry knows there is no more planning, moving, strategy, to avoid what is coming.

He just doesn't know when or the how.

As he walks down the hall which seems to be a mile long, he tries to get a happy face back to not let on what just happened.

As he walks into Sue's room, he lets Tana down and watches as she meets her new twin sisters for the first time.

A very happy moment, right then he realized, he best man up and make the best out of every second he had left.

He walked over and picked up both girls, both fast asleep. Tana just can't sit still, overwhelmed with love for her twin sisters.

He looked over at Sue who was smiling. She asks, "Well, daddy, what do you think about this? Can I surprise you or what?"

He says, "Oh yeah, that was one for the books. I cannot believe you could keep such a secret from us for six months, unbelievable."

"You are not upset with me not telling you?" with a slight frown on her face.

He smiles, then lets off a huge "Hooray", one for the books, waking both girls up.

"Now the fun begins," he says, listening to his family all talking and crying making such a racket, music to his ears.

She asks, "Well we had picked out one girl and boy name so what do you think now we have two girl names to pick out?"

"Well, I think we go with Lily for one and Elizabeth for the second."

"Sounds great to me she says."

The girls were healthy, but as twins go, they were small at first. Both girls and mom stay in the hospital for a second day to be sure all is well before being released to go home.

Meanwhile Tana and Larry have a day to themselves before picking up mommy and sisters, late the next day.

He asks Tana what she would like to do. She says, "I would like to go look at some beautiful horses out at that ranch by your office."

"Well, that can be arranged. I will call them and see if that's okay and we will make a day of it starting tomorrow morning. How's that sound?"

Tana, in anticipation of going to see the horses, couldn't sleep much that night.

Larry did not sleep at all; he kept wondering how much time he had left.

He realizes now that Sue and his approach to living life had been the right approach, but that was not ever knowing if Frank knew where they were. Now he knows and that changes everything.

He stopped looking over his shoulder, but now he needs eyes in the back of his head. Sue kept a secret from Tana and him for months, the least he could do is the same. Happy smiles, happy days, from now on. Don't look back, always forward; don't give Frank the satisfaction of knowing this is tearing Larry apart.

The next day Tana and Larry went to the horse ranch. To Tana's surprise, Larry had set it up so she could pick out a horse she liked to ride as long as she wanted.

Tana was more than thrilled. She kept on saying, "I cannot wait to have my sisters go horse riding with me, daddy."

Larry was smiling and laughing as the hours ran down to go and pick up the rest of his family.

The family was now all together for the first time at home. It was a special time for everyone.

Laughter, crying, yelling, noisy, loving every minute of it.

The house well-kept, all in order, looked like a train wreck in just a few days.

Larry always thinking ahead tells Sue, "I think what this family needs is a new puppy and a nanny."

She responds, "I understand the puppy, but what's the deal with a nanny? I can surely take care of the kids and house."

"Sue," he says, "I love you dearly. I want you to be able to spend every minute of every day with your family. I will not take no as an answer."

She says, "Well if you put it that way, why not. The house was built with a guest bedroom, bath, sitting area, so we can hire a live-in help."

"Now you're getting with the program."

Sue places an ad with full disclosure looking for a nanny. Months went by but no response.

Then one day from nowhere, she gets a letter from a gentleman that says he would love to come and help taking the nanny position. He was just recently widowed after being married for quite some years and has no other family.

She at first has her doubts, but after talking it over with Larry, they both agree, why not.

She sends him a reply that they would like to talk a bit more on the position with him if he is still interested.

He responds, "Yes that would be a possibility as soon as I finish up something that I am obligated to do, maybe a month or so, then I will contact you again to see if the position is still available and go from there."

Sue tells Larry about the gentleman's response needing some time.

Larry, being very suspicious and not to alarm Sue that this might be Frank's attempt to get information on how they are doing, tells Sue, "Why don't we stop at this point, give him time to see if he recontacts us later, then go from there." She agrees.

So on with their lives they go, Sue taking up both motherly and household duties, Larry making his company one of the top ten in Arizona for development and construction, the kids, well they just kept doing what kids do best, being kids.

Days, weeks, months go by as time does so easily, life passing out curve balls around every corner.

One typical morning, Larry gets up early like usual, makes some coffee, little pastry of some kind. Then Sue wanders out trying to get a few peaceful moments alone with Larry before the gang storms in.

They talk about the electric bill that is always too high, the food, clothing, and other essentials all growing families need.

Larry keeps saying he needs to keep getting a yard man to keep up, but down deep he enjoys trimming and mowing, making the large yards look well groomed.

But they always end up talking about the next camping vacation they will take. They all love being outdoors in the mountains.

Larry usually leaves to get to the office by eight just in case anyone needs any last-minute directions on ongoing projects.

So today was a typical morning start for everyone, mid-afternoon. Larry, not having any urgent items to attend to, decided he would take the rest of the day off, go home and spend some time with the girls. It was too early to pick up Tana from school, so he went straight home.

They lived only twenty minutes away, a short trip down a two-lane paved road.

After the short drive and making the last turn towards home, he sees a car parked down a side dirt road, the same one that was there when he passed by early this morning.

He stops and gets out of his truck, looking around as he approaches the car, close enough to see inside. Nothing appears out of place. He looks around again, scanning out as far as he can, looking for any signs of the owner. He checks and the door is unlocked, so he looks around for any information on the car, glove box empty, nothing in any side pockets.

As he is walking around the back of the car to look better on the other side, he glances at the license plate, which is not there—now that is odd.

Larry starts to get the feeling he is being watched and the fear of Frank flushes over his entire being.

He bends down to conceal himself, thinking he must make a run for his truck or do I just walk over like nothing is wrong.

He stands up, glances once more at the back of the car and walks the 30 yards back to his truck, the longest walk of his life, knowing any minute his life would or could be over.

As he approaches his truck, he notices the driver's door wide open. Thinking he shut it, he stops, then slowly approaches the truck watching for any movement at all.

He approaches the open door keeping the door between himself and the door opening for some protection.

Walking around the open door, laying on the driver's seat was an envelope.

He picks it up, sets it over on the passenger side, starts the truck and drives away.

The remaining five-minute drive lasted forever. Waiting for anything that might happen, he pulls into his driveway but stops short of going into the garage thinking. If anything were to happen with the truck, he did not want any damage to the house.

Stopping, shutting the engine off, then slowly while looking around him, he picked up the letter and opened it up.

Inside was a single sheet of paper, with very little writing that read, "Any day now I shall reap my vengeance on those that betrayed me in the past. As I said in the past, you will not know when, but your last thoughts will be, you know who."

As he gets out of his truck and walks out to the mailbox that is at the end of the driveway, he opens the mailbox, pulls out the mail, shuts the mailbox, starts walking back up the driveway, glancing around, and there a few hundred yards away is the van, the one that has been following him around for the longest time, he knows now he has little time left.

He has yet to ever let Sue know about Frank that day in the maternity ward, nor she will ever be told.

Thinking to himself he wants to be sure the girls are safe and out of harm's way, seeing Tana's summer break started last week, he comes up with a plan.

He goes to Sue and tells her, "I must work a couple days then we can take our two-week camping trip. What I would like for you to do is take the

RV, head out for the campground we always stay ahead of me getting things setup. I will follow no more than a couple of days, after I help close out this major project."

Sue responds, "We can wait and all go together. Two days more will not make any difference."

Larry, trying to get her to go without being obvious that something is wrong, just adds, "Do what you want, but I thought you girls like those outdoor arts and crafts shows that I hate, and figured you could take the girls and go bonkers for a couple days shopping."

Sue replies, "I knew you had an alternate reason, you sneak. That's a pretty good idea, that way we don't have to watch you moping around trying to act like you want to be there. Okay, we will leave tomorrow."

Larry was relieved that he now will have his family out of the way and safe.

The next day comes. Larry does his best to act like nothing is wrong, playfully teasing the girls not to spend their college funds at the craft show, kisses and hugs all around. The girls, all excited, head out for the campground.

Larry didn't want to go back into an empty house, so he walks up to the front door and locks it.

Getting into his truck, he starts driving, not knowing where he might end up.

He stops by the office, just sitting in his truck looking at the building from the parking lot.

He does the same thing to a few of his projects they had completed and some they have ongoing.

He goes by the school that Tana goes to and the hospital the twins were born.

All these places bring back memories of great days he has had with his loved ones.

The daytime now has given way to the evening hours, so he stops at the family's favorite restaurant for what he believes to be his last meal.

As he leaves the restaurant and pulls out of a very lit parking lot, he looks left, all clear, then right there sits the van.

His drive home while watching the van the entire way home was totally nerve-racking to say the least.

Larry thought to himself, I thought Frank said he always left his targets wondering who or why this has happened to them. Now in plain view, he is sending me a message that he is here, so why not just get it over.

Larry pulls into his driveway, opens the garage door, drives into the garage, stops, puts it in park, turns off his engine, and just sits there, thinking when, please be quick and fast with as little pain as possible.

He exits his truck, stops just short of closing the door and notices the van just down the street about fifty yards away.

So, this is it, Frank sitting well within any type of weapon he may choose to end my life Larry thinking.

The van positioned so a shot can be made through the passenger's window, not exposing the weapon or himself at any time.

Textbook sniper type positioning, concealment, resting point for firing, multiple easy escape routes.

Larry decides he is done. He walks out of the garage, closes it behind him, walks the long walkway to the front door in full view of what would be an easy kill shot for any professional person.

Walking and waiting to feel the burn of a bullet ripping into his body at any second.

He gets to the door, unlocks it, glances in the direction of the van, but no van. He again appears but does nothing, stalking, tormenting Larry.

He walks through the door locking it behind himself.

He takes a deep breath, thinking, maybe one more day.

The next morning Larry gets up at his usual time and goes through his ritual to go to work, minus the family.

The empty house feels cold and empty without all the kids and Sue. He looks around, thinking, well at least I have set my family to live comfortably when I am gone, both with this fine home—Sue made it a home—and the kids that make it a complete family.

Feeling good inside, he decides to head to the office to get a few items wrapped up.

The drive was very normal without any incidents. Office noise was a good for the nerves, chatting with the office personnel on the upcoming holiday season ahead, meeting with project managers to help solve situations that needed attention.

All along, he kept thinking about his girls, shopping at the craft show, waiting to see daddy show up soon. He knew how hard it was going to be for them when he was gone, nothing he could do but hope they would remember him as he hoped, a loving father and husband.

Getting late and many leaving for the weekend, he told the remaining few to go ahead on home and he would lock up.

One of the office gals told him they were expecting a package delivery within the next thirty minutes if he could wait. He responds, "Sure thing, now get out of here and have a great weekend."

Larry wonders around the office, checking out everyone's desks, some highly organized, others looking like a scrap yard after a tornado hit, smiling to himself how it takes so many different personalities to make things work out.

Larry, glancing at his watch and realizing thirty minutes had come and gone, decided to lock up and head for home.

As he starts to close the door, he pauses for a second or so. Glancing back, he shuts and locks the door.

Just before he turns around, he hears a familiar sounding horn, doesn't put it together but then to his amazement, he sees the RV coming down the road, with all the girls waving, yelling, and Sue's heavy on the horn.

The same time the delivery truck enters the parking lot in front of them.

The delivery truck pulls up, driver's side towards me.

The girls and RV are gently pulling into the driveway. Sue was always careful when driving the RV.

Watching the girls pull in, Larry sees the delivery driver stepping out of the truck with a large envelope, the delivery the office gal was expecting.

Then as he glances over the left shoulder of the delivery man, he sees the van sitting on the far side of the lot.

He reaches out to take the envelope from him asking, "Do I need to sign anything?"

He responds, "No, sir, no signing today."

Larry looks up from the envelope. There stands Frank, looking down he sees a pistol.

Larry asks, 'Thought you said your targets never know who or why?"

Frank replies, "Well seeing we have history, I thought I would make this the exception."

All things happening, Frank, my girls coming and will see me shot down, and that damn van, nothing he could do. Larry shut his eyes. A shot rang out. He flinched, waiting for the burning sensation of a bullet passing through his body, but nothing.

Larry slowly opened his eyes, Frank laid dead on the ground at Larry's feet. A bullet had struck him in the head.

Larry, frantic to see who this had done, only heard the girls screaming and running towards him. He ran over stopping them short not to let them see the man lying in a pool of blood.

Larry asks Sue to take the girls back to the RV and wait. She looked into Larry's eyes and asks, "Is that Frank on the ground?" He nods, yes.

Then she looks past Larry and sees another man coming towards them who has a rifle pointed at Larry. She screams!

Something about this man was familiar to Larry, not someone to fear, but felt more of a friend not enemy.

The man walks closer lowering his rifle; he yells out, "Everyone okay over here?"

Larry and Sue both recognized the voice, the voice so many times brought comfort and support. He asks again, "Little miss, you all okay?"

Sue replies, "We sure are now that the Sheriff back in town."

Larry and Sue couldn't believe their eyes and hearts as he strolled up.

"Larry," the Sheriff barks, "now you open that there office door and get them girls inside out of all this mess."

He walks over and places his jacket over Frank so the girls would not see.

Just like the first time they met the Sheriff, every type of law enforcement agency showed up. The most wanted man has been put down by the Sheriff.

He did as he said all along, he would protect his little miss.

After a while gone by and the removal of Frank's body, the girls came out and met the Sheriff.

Sue just could not let him go, hanging on to him like the girls do with Larry.

Larrry asks, "What the heck are you doing here?"

The Sheriff replied, "I knew when Frank got all those good FBI guys, and Fyfe, that he might come looking for you. I took an early retirement and started looking for you all. By luck, I came across someone I went to school with, who lives in Casa Grande. We got to talking one day and I mentioned I was looking for a young couple that may go by the name Sue and Larry. Said he ran into a fella that had been looking for an old girlfriend named Sue, so I did a little more research, found Larry one day and knew he would lead me to Sue, so I bought a van that was equipped for camping and started following you guys. Tana was such a fine little girl, and then later, twin sisters, so now I had an entire family to watch over, and I did make you all a promise, remember?"

Sue asks the Sheriff, "Did you see me waiving goodbye on the plane?"

"Sure did, I knew right then that no silly ass, government-run protection program was going to keep my girl safe. Funny thing, one day while I was following you guys, I was stopped, and a whole bunch of officers swarmed my van. I had a heck of a time explaining to them boys that I was not going to rob the place. Seeing I was a retired sheriff, they did finally let me go."

Larry, clearing his voice, says, "Well I am to blame for that. I saw the van following me quite often and thought it to be Frank, so I didn't want the van to follow us to Cottonwood, so I called 911 and told them there was four of you guys casing the store."

Sheriff just roared with laughter. After a minute he said, "Well I sure am glad you all are okay. Best I finish up with all these badges wearing suited fellows and get back to start my golden years."

Sue asks, "Bet your wife and kids will be happy to see you again?"

"Well, little miss, my wife passed away right before all of this first started out, have no kids or relatives, going to be a new way of life for me, for sure. Don't you fret nothing over me. You all take care now."

Sheriff walks over and gives Larry a handshake, gives him a smile, and a first-time hug, picks up Tana to give her a big bear hug and kiss on the cheek.

Tana, not even knowing the Sheriff, gave him back a hug and kiss, saying, "Thanks for protecting my mommy and daddy."

"My pleasure, sugar."

He then picks up each twin and lightly kisses their forehead saying, "Precious little darlings."

Sheriff turns to Sue, tears now running down both the Sheriff's and Sue's faces.

Sue hugs him not wanting to let go. The Sheriff says, "Now, missy, don't let on, you all will be just fine now," as she keeps hugging him.

She finally lets go, gives him a kiss on both cheeks and says, "We will never forget you."

Larry asks, "So what are your plans once you get home, Sheriff?"

Sheriff, "Well I have a pension coming, don't have a home, but a fine camping van. Guess I'll do some fishing. I did apply for a job but not sure if the position will still be open."

Larry looks at Sue, Tana, then the twins, and says, "You know, all of this might of have never happened without your help, almost like a guardian angel. How about becoming a permanent guardian angel and new member to our family? We have plenty of room at our new home. We have a nice guest quarter and can always use a good man to help run our security for our construction company."

The sheriff lowered his head. A moment went by as he slowly raised up. He had the look of a younger man would have, with tears coming from the corners of his eyes. "Well now, I guess that position for a nanny is still open."

Sue looks at him and asks, "You are the widower that applied?" smiling.

"Yes, ma'am I sure am."

"I can't think off hand of any better offer I've had in a while," he pauses and swallows hard, "so let's give it a whirl. But one thing though, no more calling me Sheriff. You must call me Grandpa Joe! "

The entire family and the Sheriff come together encircling the twins carriage.

The Sheriff looking down into the carriage, with Larry on one side and Sue on the other, Tana in front and leaning back on him. He slowly raises his huge arms to embrace his newfound family.

Sue rests her head slowly on his chest and with a sigh of relief, looks up and whispers, "Thank you."

I once heard a man tell another when he was asked a simple question,
I just want a normal life.
He replied,
There is no such thing as a normal life.
There is just life.